more than friends
a Kendrick Place novel

more than friends
a Kendrick Place novel

JODY HOLFORD

This book is a work of fiction. Names, characters, places, and incidents are the product of the author's imagination or are used fictitiously. Any resemblance to actual events, locales, or persons, living or dead, is coincidental.

Copyright © 2016 by Jody Holford. All rights reserved, including the right to reproduce, distribute, or transmit in any form or by any means. For information regarding subsidiary rights, please contact the Publisher.

Entangled Publishing, LLC
2614 South Timberline Road
Suite 109
Fort Collins, CO 80525
Visit our website at www.entangledpublishing.com.

Bliss is an imprint of Entangled Publishing, LLC. For more information on our titles, visit http://www.entangledpublishing.com/category/bliss

Edited by Stacy Abrams and Alexa May
Cover design by Melody Pond
Cover art from iStock

Manufactured in the United States of America

First Edition December 2016

To Kalie and Amy ~ I love you

*My soul whispers to me that it wishes to intertwine with yours so when the tides of life come crashing we are one–
inseparable*
Mustafa Tattan

Chapter One

It'll be fine. Just one friend asking another friend for a favor. The joyful *clang* of Christmas music was easy to hear through the closed door. Owen Burnett clenched his jaw. If things went as planned, he'd have to convince Gabby to swap out her bubble-gum pop for something more sedate. A little bit of Bing crooning "White Christmas" seemed like a good compromise.

If she agreed. Owen was mostly confident his best friend would give him exactly what he needed.

But just in case, he'd brought pizza.

In his socked feet, said pizza in hand, he took a deep breath and let himself into her apartment, kitty-corner to his, as he had a hundred times before.

"Gabs?"

"In here. Do I smell pizza?"

"Jesus, you have a bionic nose," he said over the thumping mash-up of different singers. Making his way down the hall, he arched a brow at the several boxes she had stacked in the living room, all marked "Christmas." None were unpacked.

Gabriella stood at her easel, her hand swirling colors on a palette. The canvas was a blur of dark shades blending into one another. Owen loved watching her work take shape and turn from nothing into something extraordinary. As someone who could draw only stick figures, it fascinated him. When she painted, drew, or doodled, her face would take on the emotion of whatever she was creating. And sometimes, like now, Owen got lost watching her.

A long strand of dark hair danced in front of her eyes despite her efforts to blow it out of the way. There was too much of it to ever stay tucked back completely. She'd obviously changed out of her day clothes—as an administrative assistant at a local community college, she regularly wore business casual. She hated every minute in them, and Owen couldn't blame her, as wearing what he wanted was a perk of his own job.

She smiled at him over her shoulder. "Knew it. Give me a sec, I'm starving. If I have a bionic nose, you have a sixth sense for when I need food."

Owen laughed and set the still-hot pizza on the coffee table. "Pretty easy when the answer to that is 'always.'"

He turned the music down, ignoring her protest, and went to get a couple of beers from her fridge. Napkins and beers in hand, he realized the tightness in his chest was nerves—something he never felt around Gabby. *She'll be fine with it. She'll probably think it'll be fun.* Of the two of them, she was definitely the more adventurous one. Still, he gave himself an extra moment to take a few deep breaths.

She'd settled into the corner of her couch, a slice of pizza already in hand when he walked back in. Laughing, he passed her one of the beers.

"Don't wait for me." She grinned and took a huge bite.

Owen sat beside her and pulled a slice for himself. His glasses fogged briefly when he took a bite, making Gabby smile. The corners of her eyes crinkled when she smiled at him like that, making it impossible not to grin along with her. Her easy-going, almost-always-happy personality was just one of the things that made her a great friend.

He gestured to the pile of boxes. "I heard you dragging this stuff down the hall first thing this morning. Thought for sure you'd have all your decorations up by now."

In reality, he thought the contents of the boxes would have been everywhere. He figured she'd have dug in, gotten a good start, and then been distracted. She was often hit with bursts of inspiration in the middle of something and everything else around her tended to fall away. She had no trouble working in a cluttered space.

"Maybe I was waiting for you," she said around a bite of pizza. Then she laughed at her own joke.

She knew full-well he thought Christmas was a time for overspending and chaos, how he wasn't a fan of the crowds tripling and even the prices of everyday items shooting up. Gabby enjoyed teasing him about what she called his "Scrooginess." He, in turn, liked to point out she was a cross between Pollyanna and Julie Andrews.

Gabby took a long swallow of her beer, then wiped her lips with her napkin. Owen watched her, paying more attention to her features than he had in the past—particularly her lips. His mother would love her. She was the kind of girl his family dreamed about him settling down with—the kind he couldn't have imagined being with, other than as a friend. *Best friend.* That's exactly what Gabriella Michaelson had become over the past couple years. Small moments and conversations had turned into shared pizzas while watching the Celtics. The conversations got longer and the time they spent together increased to the point where they spent more time with each other than without. They'd become part of each other's routine.

Other than work and sleep, they did most things together. Sometimes their friend Brady—who also lived in the building—joined them, but whether he did or didn't, Owen and Gabby were comfortable. *Which makes this not a big deal.*

"Do I have pizza on my face?" When she touched her cheeks, checking for sauce, he saw the dried paint on her nails and fingers.

Shoot. He'd been staring. Owen laughed. "No. Just paint, as usual. What are you working on?"

Gabby pulled her bottom lip between her teeth, then looked down. She spoke low, a sign that she was nervous and had something important to share. "I got asked to do an exclusive showing in the New Year. Five pieces at the Carter Klein Gallery."

"Gabby! Wow!" He set his beer down and, beaming at her, grabbed her by both arms to yank her close. The Klein Gallery was a big deal, and to be asked to do an exclusive was even bigger. She more than deserved the break. "This is awesome!"

She gave a carefree laugh and hugged him back, her chin resting on his shoulder. He'd hugged her before, but he couldn't remember ever being so aware of the sweet smell of her hair or the way her body fit against his. It felt comfortable. Natural. His family wouldn't question the relationship if it were this easy to hold her. And why wouldn't it be? She was Gabby. *His* Gabby. She'd have no issue with what he was about to propose.

He winced at the word "propose." If his mother had her way, he'd be down on one knee before his thirtieth birthday in January, which was why he hoped his idea would hold her off. She'd see he and Gabby were great together. She didn't have to know they were only buddies—too different to be anything else to each other. Gabby would probably slap him for even thinking otherwise.

She sat back, shifting so she was on her own cushion again. "Thanks. I'm pretty pumped, but it's short notice. They called around nine, right after I'd brought the boxes up, and I couldn't wait to get started," she said, gesturing to the canvas.

Her smooth skin was tinged pink with the excitement of her news, and her brown eyes literally sparkled. When he'd met her a couple years ago, he'd thought she was attractive in a disheveled kind of way, but hadn't paid close attention. He'd had Vanessa-vision; a rare condition where he believed he'd found the right girl based on her perfectly coifed hair and immaculate style. It had taken him far too long to figure out how imperfect their relationship was.

Gabby tilted her head and smacked his shoulder, snapping him out of his own thoughts. "Okay, for real, why are you looking at me like that?"

Unaccustomed to the flurry of nerves playing in his stomach, he picked at the label on his beer bottle and kept his voice nonchalant. "I'm actually glad you haven't gone Christmas-crazy yet." Owen chuckled when she scoffed.

Grabbing another piece of pizza, Gabby leaned back on her side of the couch. "Really? Did you have a change of heart, Mr. Grinch? You wanna get all Christmassy with me?" She fluttered her lashes exaggeratedly.

Owen's stomach tightened. He set his beer down harder than he meant to, making foam rise up a bit. Pulling it back, he sipped off the top, set it down more carefully, and leaned forward, his forearms resting on his knees as he met her gaze. "Yes, actually."

Gabby laughed and continued to chew her food. She stretched her feet out, crossing her ankles on the coffee table. His eyes wandered the length of her legs to her ankles. Had he ever noticed how delicate her bones were? Like a dancer's. *What's wrong with you? Focus. Just ask her.*

Her brows furrowed as she looked down at his hand.

"What's the catch? You hate Christmas—which doesn't get you out of buying me a gift, by the way."

He groaned, realizing he'd need to hit the mall for more presents—not Gabby's; he'd had that for a while. It was too late to shop online and be sure of delivery. He'd probably need to go to the grocery store as well. He didn't have enough food for six people for the holidays. Owen stood abruptly and bumped the table, jostling Gabby's legs. She startled and stared up at him.

"What the hell, O?"

Owen ran his hands through his hair. He needed a trim, but his barber was on vacation. No way was he trying someone new. Better long than hacked off. He paced a little, then pulled off his black-framed glasses, using the act of cleaning them on the tail end of his button up shirt to align the words properly in his head. It was a simple proposal. No—proposition.

When he looked back at Gabby, she'd put her pizza down and watched him with a wariness he didn't often see in her eyes. "What's going on?"

"My parents are coming for Christmas. Actually, my parents and my sister." He took a deep breath. The pressure in his chest returned. "And my aunt."

Gabby's eyes went wide right before she burst into laughter. She wrapped her arms around herself and laughed until he saw tears gathering at the corner of her eyes.

Owen glared and put his hands on his hips. Of course she'd find humor in this. "Shut it. It's not funny." It was true—there was nothing funny about the thought of his family coming to stay with him for a week or what his mom had shared with him, but Gabby's laugh always got to him, and a smile crept through. Dammit, she had the best laugh. He picked up one of her funky throw pillows from a chair and tossed it at her head.

Gabby ducked and the pillow fell to the floor. She shook her head and wiped her hands on a napkin. "Not funny?

Which part isn't funny? The part where you, King of Clean—Master of Order—has to share your apartment? With *four other people*. Or is it the fact that you hate Christmas and tried to get out of it by telling them you had to work—which I *told* you would backfire—and now you're hosting it. Sorry, O. This is more than funny. It is serves-you-right hilarious!"

Hands back on his hips, he continued to glower at her, but she only laughed harder, like she was immune to him.

"Stop. Laughing. I don't *hate* Christmas. Well, maybe the malls. My mom doesn't know the meaning of 'small get-together' or 'family only.' I didn't want another Christmas like the last one. People I don't know everywhere. They played Charades, Gabby. The *holiday* version."

She nodded as she tried not to giggle, her teeth digging into her bottom lip. As always, it was bare—she rarely wore makeup. Not that she needed it. She was striking without. How had he never noticed how full her lips were? Drawing further attention to them, she pressed her lips together and scrubbed her hands over her face. Her muffled laughter came in small bursts. When Owen growled and stalked to the window, nearly tripping over two of the boxes, she jumped off the couch and launched herself at him.

Her arms wrapped around him from behind, her cheek pressing into his back. "I'm sorry. It has elements of funny, but I can see why you wouldn't think so." She took a few deep breaths, then let them out. "Okay. We've got this. You can borrow a few of my decorations, and when they're not looking you can sneak over here to escape the noise and mess. I'll even try to tidy up."

She moved around so she stood in front of him. With her hand, she pushed at his shoulder playfully and gave him a sweet Gabby smile, her attempt to make peace.

He knew from the way her lips quivered she was still working to keep the laughter at bay, but she held strong.

"When are they coming? I can't wait to meet them. I told you your mom wasn't going to deal well with you not going home for Christmas." Tucking her chin down, she walked past him and began cleaning their dinner mess.

The room was too warm. Owen looked at the window, the frost decorating the outside corners, and thought of opening it. A tree filled the window directly across from Gabby's in the neighboring building. She hated that her place didn't have a view. *Which is what makes this a great idea.* The apartment was really stuffy. *Do it, already.* "Yeah. About that. Remember when I said I told them I couldn't get away because of work?" He faced her, knowing he couldn't avoid her eyes when he asked.

Pizza box in hand, she nodded, her smile quieter. "Yeah?"

"My mom was pressing so hard and I was feeling guilty. So I...I told her I'd finally met someone. *The* one. I told her I couldn't come home because I didn't want to leave at the most romantic time of the year. I thought she'd accept it and back off," Owen said. He looked down at the carpet, digging his toes into the fibers. His own apartment was wall-to-wall hardwood—which he knew Gabby coveted. She mentioned it every time they hung out at his place.

"Oh my God, Owen. You're an idiot," Gabby said.

His head snapped up and he started to argue, but since he still needed her, badly, he figured it was best to stay on her good side.

Besides, she was right. He was an idiot.

Time to go all in. "There's more."

Gabby's sweater started to slip off her shoulder and Owen's eyes followed, drawn to the spaghetti strap of the purple tank top underneath. Her shoulders rose and fell with her deep sigh.

"Tell me."

"They're coming to meet her. That's *why* they're coming.

They want to meet the woman I'm in love with, so in love that I can't make it home for Christmas this year." Last year had been such a gong show. On Christmas Eve his mother had invited every one of her theater students for an impromptu sing-along.

Gabby shook her head, her eyes still smiling, this time with empathy and warmth. "Ouch. So what're you going to do? You're not even dating anyone. Where are you going to come up with your dream girl before they get here?"

He held her gaze and watched the laughter slip from her eyes. She tilted her head, scrunching her brows as she started putting the unsaid pieces together one second at a time. Her eyes widened. Gabby gripped the pizza box so tight the cardboard creaked. She took a step back, bumping into a pile of Christmas ornaments and stumbling. Owen didn't catch the pizza box when it fell, but he managed to grip her arms and stop her from following it down.

She looked at the box, which had landed sideways but stayed closed, and then up at him. "Me? I'm supposed to be the girl you love? *The* girl?" Her voice was nearly a whisper, and though he thought he knew almost every one of her expressions, he couldn't decipher the one she wore now.

He gave a half laugh, steadying her, then stepping back. "Well, you're *a* girl. One who knows me better than anyone. And I love you, so it's not a total lie," he said.

Gabby's face contorted and turned an interesting shade of red. She picked up the pizza box with jerky movements. "You love me?" The squeak in her voice didn't match the fire in her eyes.

Owen shrugged. Again, he rubbed the back of his neck with one hand. Had they never said that to each other? Probably not. Some things weren't necessary to say between best friends. Right? "Well, yeah. We're best friends. Of course I love you. Don't you love me?"

He wasn't sure how her face could go from red to white so quickly. With a shrill laugh, she yelled, "No!"

Owens throat constricted. "Hey!" *What the hell? We're best friends.*

She piled the discarded and extra napkins on top of the box and began to babble as she walked to the kitchen. "No. I mean I don't love-love you, but of course I love you, like… like a best friend. But me? I'm totally not your type and your parents will know that. They'll never believe you'd fall for someone like me. I'm messy and disorganized. I didn't even remember to do my taxes until the last minute, after you nagged me. Hell, then I just got you to do them for me. I don't even separate my lights and darks. I'm actually the opposite of everything you have on your list of what makes a perfect woman."

Owen stilled. The air had been sucked out of the room. "How do you know about my list? Were you on my computer?"

She turned to stare at him, her mouth hanging open a little. With a shaky laugh, she tossed the pizza box onto the counter. His fingers itched to pick up the scattered napkins, to pile them neatly.

"You have an actual list? Oh my God. I was being facetious."

His face heated. "Oh. Of course I don't. I was joking." Stepping forward, he bent his knees so they were eye to eye. Gabby twisted a napkin between her fingers. He took it from her hands. "Gabby, please. I need you."

She winced. "Just tell them the truth. Tell them you didn't want to come home to all the hustle and bustle of the holidays. They're your family; it'll be okay. You know how I feel about lying."

He did know, and it made him a lousy friend to ask this of her, but he'd already tried to think of another way and couldn't.

"I can't, Gabs. My mom cried when I told her. She was so happy I'd found someone. Then she called this morning and said they'd changed their plans and they'd be here in a few days."

Gabby paced the kitchen, making the space between them feel too small. "Okay, fine, she'll be disappointed and maybe even a little mad. But you can tell her."

Owen's breath caught in his lungs when he remembered his mom's words. "It's not just about disappointing them. My aunt Patty is having a hard year."

Gabby stopped pacing. "Hard how?"

He hadn't wanted to play the sympathy card, but he wouldn't lie to Gabby of all people. He hadn't actually intended to lie to anyone. "She and my uncle are divorcing. She's nearing seventy and starting her life over."

Gabby's face contorted. She so easily empathized with others' pain. "I'm sorry. That's very sad. But still…"

"I tried to tell my mom the truth, but she started going on about how good it would be for Patty to be with family, to see me in love and have something so great to celebrate. Then she said maybe her sister's Christmas could be salvaged after all."

Gabby groaned.

"How could I tell my mom it wasn't true? That I made something up to stay home? I feel like a jerk, but I can't tell her. Please, Gabby."

Shaking her head, she began to pace again, her breath coming in short bursts. "Please what? Pretend to be your girlfriend for a week? No one will buy it. Half the time I'm not even sure you know I'm female."

What? Sure, he didn't think of her *that* way, but he wasn't blind. She was definitely female. It's not like he hadn't noticed she had…breasts and curves and…damn, now he was thinking of both those things. He stared down at the ground, suddenly and uncomfortably aware of her…femininity more than ever before.

Even without looking at her, he could picture the elegant curve of her neck and the show of skin where her sweater hung loose, her gorgeous hair that made him think of rich chocolate and her pretty face with her endless, open smiles. Just because they were friends didn't mean he was completely oblivious. Looking up, he saw she'd turned away, her hands gripping the counter.

He might not have thought too much about it, but he could damn well see she was a woman. And he didn't need that knowledge or awareness getting in the way. He watched the rise and fall of her back, and then she turned and walked away from him. In the living room, she took over his spot by the window, staring out at the inky black sky. The stars were like little cutouts of light peeking in.

He leaned against the arch separating the living room and kitchen. "Look at me." He waited until she did. "I know I'm asking a lot. It'll probably be awkward. My family is loud and messy. Messier than you, if you can imagine." She tried to scowl at him, but it had no heat, and that felt like a small victory. "I know you hate to lie and I hate asking you to. But you love Christmas and so do they. I don't want to wreck it for them. It's not a big deal—a few days with my family and no one will know otherwise. I'm asking you to help me and in return, I…I'll give you something I know you've been wanting for a long time."

Because he was staring at her so intently, he saw the way her eyes darkened and her chest flushed. Trying to avoid looking at her breasts, he caught her gaze again. Owen walked across the room once more, the scent of her shampoo catching him off-guard, kicking him in the gut with the delicious sweetness of it. Like candy or gingerbread. Maybe Christmas wasn't so bad.

"What's that?" she whispered, folding her arms so one hand rested on her biceps and the other rested against her mouth.

Closing the distance between them, he reached out a hand and stroked her hair. Her hands dropped to her sides. He trailed his finger down her jaw to her chin and tilted her head up to meet his gaze. She really did have gorgeous eyes. Knock-a-man-on-his-ass eyes that were watching him, full of an emotion he couldn't name.

He smiled, bent his knees again, and then pinched her chin gently between his thumb and forefinger. "My apartment."

Chapter Two

Gabby's heart beat like a hummingbird's wings. The room was like a sauna, and the pressure in her chest was bordering on painful. She'd imagined this moment more times than she could count. Owen—the sexy-if-somewhat-nerdy tech wizard, her next-door neighbor, her *best* friend—standing close enough to breathe the same air, telling her he wanted her to be his girlfriend. Not once, in all her extremely detailed daydreams, had it gone down like this.

The heat of his fingers continued to singe her skin and his eyes burned into her, making it impossible to hide her surprise. She knew he was oblivious to her feelings. If he knew what she felt—the depth of what she kept locked up inside for him—he'd snatch his hand back in an instant.

He was *killing* her.

"Say something, Gabs." He dropped his hands and shoved them in his back pockets. His glasses made his green eyes seem bigger, more intense. He watched her closely and she knew the subtle way he pursed his lips together was a sign of his nervousness. Owen was rarely nervous. He was steady and calm and in control. She knew so much about him—too much. He took his coffee with sugar and milk, not cream. He loved to throw on his shirt right out of the dryer so it warmed his skin. He slept in only one day of the week, preferred milk chocolate over dark, and hated any sort of fruit in muffins, even though he loved fruit. He disliked Christmas and "chick flicks," but would tolerate both for her.

And now she knew he loved her, in the safest way possible. The most platonic, means-nothing way he could. Which, in her books, was the same as not at all. *You can't have everything.*

Biting the inside of her cheek, she sidestepped him, rubbing her chin where he'd pinched it like he was an older brother or uncle. Or friend. She couldn't talk while he was touching her and looking at her with his eyes all intense. "Your family isn't stupid. You're nearly thirty years old. It's silly to hide the truth. They know you, so obviously they know you don't like the noise and huge gatherings that they enjoy. Adding more lies isn't going to make things easier." *On either of us.*

She gathered her paint supplies to keep her hands busy. She wasn't sure what she'd been about to paint anyway, but putting anything on paper or canvas soothed her. Before he'd walked in, Gabby's biggest concern was convincing herself she was good enough to be part of the Klein Gallery showing. That seemed easy compared to thinking about being Owen's pretend girlfriend, though the thought of being surrounded by a family tempted her down to her core. She loved Christmas, but it was a hard time of the year and more often than not reminded her she was alone.

Owen's voice was gentle, like the comfort of his arms during one of their hugs. "Trust me, it will definitely make things easier. Come on, it's not such a big deal. You get to watch me suffer through all the Christmas celebrations you love, you get to meet my family, and you get to have my apartment. You are winning in this scenario."

God. His apartment. It wasn't *him,* but it was every bit as beautiful. In a different way, of course. She couldn't stand still. Grabbing her brushes, she walked past him, avoiding his gaze, and went back to the kitchen to clean them. And put some space between them. It was too hard to breathe in the same room where he'd said he loved her. As a friend. Later, she'd relive the moment and fantasize that he'd meant it in an entirely different way.

Pushing the thought away, she latched on to another. "I don't get it. What do you mean I get your apartment?"

Owen leaned a hip against the counter as she warmed the water. "I mean you've wanted it since you moved in, and now I'm willing to trade with you."

She slanted her gaze toward him, frowning. "You'll just trade? I get the hardwood floors, corner unit, and wall of perfect natural lighting, and you'll move into this dungeon?"

"Dungeon" wasn't a fair term. Each of the eighteen units in the building was lovely and elegant. A cross of old-school charm with mostly present-day building code regulations. Kendrick Place was not considered a luxury apartment building, but it was completely charming and full of character. Like so many great buildings in Boston, it had history and presence. It had been a shipping warehouse long ago. One man had bought it, moved into one of the container rooms, and spent his life turning it into rental spaces one apartment at a time.

The main floor had a multi-purpose room, a fitness room, and a huge lobby. The basement held the storage and boiler rooms. During the last World War, when the building had been used to ship contents overseas, the storage room had been one of the assembly-line rooms. In addition to loving the story behind the building, Gabby felt it was in a nice area close to everything she needed. It was elegant without being stuffy, and the four corner units on each floor were an artist's dream. Aside from the views of the Boston skyline towering over the water, the units were far more spacious, with open layouts and actual floor to ceiling windows. The light pouring in made Gabby feel like she was outside without the direct glare of the sunlight. She had a unit on the opposite side of the place, so she faced another building instead of the courtyard fountain or the city.

Owen set out a towel for her brushes and nodded. "Straight-up trade. You move your stuff into my place, I move mine into yours. After the holidays, of course. For now, I was thinking we'd kind of blend our stuff so it looked like we've been sharing both spaces. You know, because we're so in love we haven't even dealt with the logistics of living space yet," he said.

His laughter nicked her heart. He thought it was funny—the idea of them being in love. He had no idea. He was the smartest man she knew and so bloody stupid she wanted to smack him.

Instead, she took another deep breath. "I don't know. It's a ridiculous trade. Why would you offer this?" She knew she was stalling. He was never going to love her the way she did him, so this might be her only chance to be this kind—the girlfriend kind—of close to him.

He reached out a hand and squeezed her shoulder. Brief. Barely a touch. Certainly nothing…sexual. But Gabby felt that touch down to her toes like she'd plugged in the toaster with wet hands. She scrubbed the paint from the sink, leaning into it, trying to put all her strength into getting out the spots. Just like that, he'd changed things. Now every touch was electric when she'd worked so hard to ignore the sensations his fingers on her skin caused. He was free with his shoulder nudges, high fives, and side hugs, so she'd learned not to read into them. Now, that felt impossible. She bit her lip so she didn't sigh out loud.

"Because I know you want it. Besides, you spend more time at my apartment than yours, anyway. You'll make better use of the space."

She scrunched her shoulders, scrubbed harder, the feel of his hand still imprinted on her skin. Realizing the sink was almost sparkling, she tossed the rag on the counter and dried her hands. Restlessness coursed through her body like it had replaced all her blood.

Gabby opened the fridge, pulled out a soda, and held it up for Owen. When he shook his head—no caffeine in the evening for him—she closed the fridge and popped the top of her can. "If you never loved it anyway, why did you take it?"

He looked down at her floor and mumbled, "Vanessa."

Gabby hid her growl at the sound of his ex's name by taking a sip of soda. Tall, blond, perfect Vanessa, who looked every bit as good on paper as she did in person. Owen had dumped her more than a year ago, but Gabby hadn't stopped measuring herself against what she knew was Owen's image of an ideal woman. Basically, the complete opposite of Gabby. At five-foot two, with generously rounded hips, long, tumbling hair that sometimes looked a little wild, and an eclectic sense of style that often favored comfort and practicality over name brands, Gabby was no match for Owen's tastes. It wasn't until Owen had dumped Vanessa that he and Gabby had gotten close.

While she was happy Vanessa was gone, she found it sad that Owen had ended a relationship because he didn't want to have children. He talked of the future, but never mentioned having a family. Not once had he ever spoken fondly about one day being a dad. Gabby had never asked him outright if that was the only reason, and she could certainly think of dozens of others, but it was the only one that made sense to her. Otherwise, why would he let go of his ideal candidate?

Whatever the reason, Gabby knew that eventually, he'd find a woman who was as perfect on the inside as she was out.

She set her soda down on the counter and went back to her brushes to dry them. She didn't like leaving them wet. She squeezed them harder than normal and watched the water drip into the sink. "Of course. Boston Barbie would only want the best."

Owen laughed and clapped her on the back. Like Gabby was some sort of kid sister. All the innocent touches meant nothing to him. *And everything to me.* With him standing so close, she had no choice but to breathe in the scent of his soap, his cologne. Him. She'd recognize his scent in a crowded room with her eyes closed. It was imprinted in her senses.

"Boston Barbie. That's cute. Come on, Gabs. Please? You wanted to meet my parents. You'll love them and they'll adore you. We're spending Christmas together, anyway." He poked her shoulder, and even that was like a pressure-point of awareness. *Who knew the shoulder could be so sensitive?*

Her voice pitched slightly because she knew she was giving in. "This is so crazy. What about after Christmas? When they find out. Because they *will* find out." She knew better than anyone where half-truths could lead. That particular lesson had flipped her life upside down.

One lie. Two deaths.

Owen straightened, and all the playfulness left his tone. "This is different. You need to stop blaming yourself. Your parents' deaths are not your fault," he said softly. Easy for him to say. He hadn't been the one to sneak out of the house at sixteen after promising his parents he wouldn't go to a party. She'd feigned illness and said she was going to bed early, and when they'd checked on her and she hadn't been in her room, they'd gone searching for her. Owen was right—the drunk driver hitting them was not her fault. But if she hadn't lied, if she hadn't broken her promise, they wouldn't have been in the car.

Owen pulled the brush from her hand and set it down, then tugged her close, his arms tightening around her, like he was trying to absorb the pain he knew she felt when she was missing her parents. But being in his arms now was almost as difficult as thinking about them without despair. She pushed away. *When in doubt, pace.*

"You're sure your family will fall for this?" The protest was weak, even to her own ears. *No surprise.* There was nothing she wouldn't do for him. And as a consolation prize, when they stopped pretending, she'd have the most kick-ass space to create five beautiful pieces that might finally secure her place in the tight-knit group of ready-to-be-known Boston artists.

"Why wouldn't they? It's one week. They're coming in a few days. My mom mentioned the twenty-third. They're leaving before New Year's because they're hosting an improv night at their studio." Right. His parents were actors and acting teachers. Maybe there was more of them in Owen than he realized. He sounded almost *into* the idea of taking on the role of her fake boyfriend. He gestured between them with his hands. "We know each other as well as any couple, so really, all we have to work on is…" Owen's words trailed off. His cheeks turned a cute shade of pink and he stepped back from Gabby.

Interesting. Her pulse sped up. Had he only just realized what the charade would entail? *Oh, Owen.* "Work on what, O?"

His hand went to the back of his neck, another tell. He glanced around the room, eyes bouncing from one object to the next. Anywhere but at her. "Well, we should… I mean, a couple would…in a real relationship a couple would—"

Her grin stretched her cheeks. *Hmm.* "Have sex?" Gabby offered. Even saying the words sent sparks zipping through her blood.

Owen's eyes widened impossibly, and a strange, garbled sound came from his throat. "What? No! I mean, yes, they would. But no," he said. He came closer but didn't touch her. The red of his cheeks practically glowed. "I would never use you like that. You know that. I would never expect that we would do...*that*. I just meant, like kiss and hold hands or something. God."

Gabby bit her lower lip because she knew he wouldn't appreciate her laughter. Of course he wouldn't expect *that*. Especially not with her. A gentleman to the core, he would only take his deception so far. And apparently he saw her as the female equivalent of a stuffed bear. *Cute and cuddly.*

But this could be her chance to test things out between them in terms of chemistry. If they had none, she was worrying for nothing. He might be a really lousy kisser. He could, quite possibly, be the worst kisser in the entire Boston area. In the universe, perhaps. Maybe he was all teeth and tongue with absolutely no finesse. If he was and there were zero sparks between them, this...this spell he had on her could be broken and she'd never want him physically again. Years from now she'd laugh about how she'd thought Owen Burnett was the one.

Maybe she only *thought* she loved him. She spent so much time with him; they laughed at each other's jokes and felt comfortable in each other's space, so naturally she thought herself crazy about him. Though she did spend a fair amount of time with their mutual friend, Brady, and nothing like this had come up. She couldn't imagine kissing him the way she often pictured with Owen. But if there were no sparks between them, it would make things easier. Not just what he was asking of her, but her life and their relationship. She could be his best friend without spending nights fearing the time he'd bring the next perfect woman home and finally say, "This is the one for me, Gabby." And then he'd probably ask her to be his best man. Because, regardless of what he said, Owen sometimes forgot that he was best friends with a girl.

He pushed his adorable glasses up his straight nose. No curves or bends from sports for her Owen. He liked watching them but didn't play anything without a controller as far as she knew.

Genuine regret tainted his voice, stabbing her in the heart. "I'm sorry. I didn't think about how awkward this would be for you. I was thinking of how easy it would be, what with our friendship, to convince my parents that we're together. I'm more comfortable with you than any woman I've ever known, so I didn't think about the...more intimate aspects of a relationship."

Of course he hadn't. She was his teddy bear. Why would he?

Owen cleared his throat. "Maybe this isn't such a great idea. I don't want to wreck things between us and I can see asking you to...well, offer intimacy in any form..."

Oh no. He isn't backing out before I find out if my attraction has any basis. What if she never got another shot? Feeling a surge of power and the familiar, always-present desire, Gabby stepped closer to Owen. His being so nervous leveled the playing field. "You can say *kiss* again, you know. I'm not scared of the word."

She put her hands on his chest, feeling the warmth of him under her fingers. His heartbeat was racing, and the knowledge gave her another boost of confidence. "You're such a prude sometimes. Just talking about making out or sex and you get flustered. You're sure you're not a virgin, right?" She laughed at the expression on his face.

Scowling at her, he gripped her wrists but didn't move her hands. "I am not a prude. Or a virgin, thank you very much. Just because I have respect for you—just because I'm not some...some wild exhibitionist, like the last clown *you* dated, doesn't mean I'm a prude."

The flip-flopping of her stomach, combined with the scent of Owen's aftershave and their conversation, was making Gabby's head spin.

Be logical. He loves logic. "You're right. If we're going to convince your family, we have to seem natural. Obviously we can be in each other's space." She looked down to where he was still holding her wrists, then met his gaze through lowered lashes. "But a couple in love would kiss and touch without thought." She hadn't meant to lower her voice. The song had ended and the quiet before the next one echoed around them, making their combined breaths seem louder.

Owen looked at her lips, then licked his own. "So you'll do it?" His voice was rough, like the words took effort to form.

Her fingers curled into the cotton of his dress shirt. "Well, I do really want your apartment."

His breathing hitched, then grew louder, and she felt the rise and fall of his chest. She stepped closer until there was no space between them, only cloth. Goose bumps tickled her arms.

He cleared his throat. "Right. The apartment. It's a good trade. And it's only a week."

Their noses were nearly touching. "A week is nothing. A week pretending to love you? I can do that." If she could spend the last several months pretending she *didn't* love him, the opposite would be a breeze.

His smile was too wide…too forced. Good. She didn't want to be the only jittery one. He nodded. "Of course you can. We'd be spending all our time together anyway. So the only thing that'll be different is—"

"The kissing," Gabby said, finishing his sentence. "And the presence of your family during said kisses, of course."

"Right. My family." She went up on her tiptoes. His nose touched hers and his hands stilled, he released her wrists so his fingers could trail their way to her upper arms. Was he holding her steady or anchoring himself? She didn't really care, as long as he didn't let go.

"If you want this to work, you'll need to feel comfortable kissing and touching me." Gabby wasn't sure which side of her brain was winning—the side that hoped he'd be a horrible enough kisser to finally squash the feelings she had for him or the side that wanted to smash her mouth against his and see if it was everything she'd dreamed it would be.

"Within reason," he said, his voice cracking slightly.

Gabby swallowed her groan. Reason was Owen's constant companion. Right up there with lists, spreadsheets, and his top ten organizational tips every bachelor should know. What she wouldn't give to kiss the *reason* right out of him.

She licked her lips. "Absolutely. Only within reason."

His lips hovered, and Gabby had to stop herself from yanking him closer. She could taste his breath and wanted more. She wanted to run her lips along his skin and inhale the scent of his soap, to consume him. She wanted to make him forget reason. Forget everything but her.

But before she could do that, Owen kissed her. His mouth touched hers tentatively, sweetly, his fingers flexing on her skin. Gabby's lips parted when Owen tilted his head. One of her hands wandered up his chest, around the back of his neck, and any thought of reason or pretending vanished. This moment, the feel of his mouth on hers, finally, was more real than anything she'd ever felt. Straining against him, she pulled him closer and kissed him with all the longing she'd been swallowing down since she realized, months ago, that he owned her heart.

One of Owen's hands moved to her hair, tangling in it as he returned her kiss without the restraint she'd expected. *God. His lips.* The way his mouth moved over hers was the opposite of comfortable. It was hot and seductive and made her feel like there was no way to get close enough. That didn't stop her from trying. When his tongue touched hers, Gabby gave in completely, wrapping both arms around his neck and taking everything she wanted. Owen's other hand moved to the small of her back, pulling her so close only air could fit between them. Every part of her lined up perfectly with every part of him.

She wondered if someone could go into shock from sensation overload.

When she could no longer breathe, Gabby leaned back. Had the room tilted, or was it just her? Owen's forehead touched hers, his eyes fluttering open slowly. Her pulse sped as she tried to find some calm, grateful his breathing was uneven as well.

He tapped her nose with his index finger and winked. "I don't think convincing them will be a problem," Owen said, his voice light and fun. "Not such a prude after all, huh?"

Gabby's heart cracked, splintering right up the middle. She could almost hear it tearing in two. Kissing him had been an epically bad idea. Now she knew exactly what she was missing. That spark and fire that curled in her stomach, the same feeling she got when she created something astounding on canvas, had spread through her entire body, claiming her heart, her soul, while they kissed.

And Owen's thoughts had been on his plan. *Because you aren't his type.* And she never would be. The next week might possibly kill her, or at least demolish her heart.

But at least she'd get the apartment.

When the week was over and the New Year came, she could lock herself inside it and look out, through-tear stained eyes, at the perfect view. She could use the natural lighting to create what would likely be the best work of her life. All great art came from heartache, right?

And Owen's easy smile, so unaffected by what they'd just shared, was heartache personified.

Chapter Three

Owen loved working from home. There were times when he had two computer screens going, his laptop open, and a phone pressed to his ear while he texted on his cell. It felt like running some sort of cool command station instead of being systems technician for a company that implemented and provided retail point of sales systems for a variety of stores. After the staff was trained on the systems and they launched to the public, he became the go-to guy for any issues. Well, he and his team.

And there were *always* issues. Because as much as the world relied on technology, the people creating it were not infallible.

He was finishing up the last of his emails before closing for the holiday. The day after Christmas was huge, with thousands of calls coming into the call center being routed to the various techs. Fortunately, he had time banked and a great rapport with his boss, so he'd been able to redirect his projects to accommodate his family's spur-of-the-moment visit. Owen supervised over a dozen support techs, did trouble-shooting online and on the phone, helped launch new systems, and—best of all—never had to leave his house. Short of working next to Bill Gates, it was his dream job.

He popped the last bite of his ham sandwich in his mouth, then brushed the crumbs off his shirt and into his hand as much as he could. Gabby had given the shirt to him. In large, white letters, it read #*Dork*. He laughed, taking his plate to the sink and grabbing his handheld vacuum. As much as he'd like to deny it, thinking of Gabby made his skin feel too tight.

She'd agreed to his plan and eventually even seemed okay with it. In fact, she'd seemed more than okay with kissing him. He'd had to cover his shock and immediate arousal by backing away and making a joke. He had *not* seen that coming. But then again, she was a beautiful woman he cared for, and he hadn't been in a relationship, physical or otherwise, in quite some time.

"Perfectly normal," he told himself, closing down the laptop. Gabby was supposed to pop over with a few of her things before she left for work. She'd be on vacation after today, so they had plenty of time to get themselves organized. Owen had made a list of what he needed to do and what they needed to get done together to make this situation work. He'd already moved some of his clothes around in his closet and cleared out a drawer in his bathroom. He'd told his mother they were practically living together because they couldn't get enough of each other. Owen hadn't planned on having to prove it.

He checked his watch. Was Gabby even awake? He hoped so; she had to be at work soon. She was bringing over some books and movies, things that could be left around and provide proof of her presence. Not that there wasn't already proof. He grinned and picked up her GAP sweater from the end of the couch and went to hang it in his closet.

Guilt gnawed at his stomach, knowing he was lying to his

family, but for the time being, it was better than adding more bad news to his aunt's worries and troubles. His family was great. He loved them and enjoyed visiting with them…for limited timeframes. They were just so damn pushy. And loud. And theatrical. How he'd come from a family of risk-taking, over-enthusiastic performers had always stumped him.

His father and mother were college sweethearts who both graduated from the theater department at a small college just outside Boston. Now, they taught side by side at a theater school in New Jersey. His older sister, Ophelia—as if that name didn't say everything—was a struggling actress who paid her rent with voice-overs and small extra roles. He spent most of his childhood wondering where he fit in.

His mother hounded him about finding the right woman to settle down with and thought he was "uptight" and "too damn picky," but Owen figured the person he spent the rest of his life with should meet the right criteria. It wasn't his fault that, so far, no woman had. Having particular tastes and expectations did not make him difficult. It made him discerning, and it grated on his nerves when they said differently. Ophelia hadn't settled down and found her other half, so why were they always hounding him?

Besides, it wasn't like he didn't date. He just didn't tell his mother about every woman who caught his interest. Owen got stuck for a moment trying to remember the last time he'd wanted to go on a date. "Doesn't matter," he said aloud. He was her youngest and she worried. If it had been just his parents and his sister, he would have gone home, maybe even brought Gabby so she wouldn't be alone. But if he'd gone, he knew it would have been a festive circus like it had been last year. This was about the only way he'd get a small family Christmas.

The washing-machine timer *buzzed* and Owen transferred his clothes before deciding that Gabby was operating in her own time zone and needed a nudge. Time to go get his pretend girlfriend settled before his family showed up. He chuckled to himself. Maybe this would be fun. His family liked drama, and now he was finally going to give them a show.

When he swung the door open, he froze. Jake, the building superintendent, leaned against Gabby's open doorframe. He'd been their building manager for the two years they'd both lived here. When Owen had shown up to put a deposit on a place with Vanessa in tow, Jake had just been telling Gabby there were two people and two apartments. He'd been obvious about checking out both Gabby and Vanessa and even then, Owen had wanted to deck him. Once Jake brought up the difference in the apartments, he'd waited, like he expected the women to wrestle for it or something. When no one offered a solution, Jake had tossed a coin to make the decision. Owen always tried to avoid him, since punching someone wasn't his style, but Jake tempted him to give it a shot.

Now, Jake was eyeing Gabby in her thin tank top and checkered pajama bottoms. It turned Owen's stomach more than it usually did, and his fists clenched. The guy hit on anything that moved and did a terrible job of managing the place. When the tenants needed something, they just called the right professional and billed the owner.

"Hey, O. I was just heading over," Gabby said. Her voice and eyes were still sleepy, her hair escaping the haphazard bun she had it in. He'd seen her like this dozens of times. They'd once gotten up at four a.m. to watch an Olympic hockey game. Why, this morning, did the sight of her grip his heart like it was in Iron Man's fist? His vision clouded slightly, and then he was stalking across the hall, like he wasn't even in charge of his own body, stepping between them, making Jake back up.

Gabby's eyes widened, becoming more awake. He was doing her a favor, getting Jake out of her personal space. That was all. She seemed surprised at how much of her space Owen was taking up. Better him than Jake, though.

Shoving his hands in his pockets, Jake laughed and said, "You two are totally banging. Guys and girls are never just friends. Not when the chick looks like you." He gave her a once-over and Owen had to work at pressing down his anger.

Gabby's body tensed, and Owen gripped her arm to stop her from launching herself at their super. She froze and just glared at him. "It's called dating or being in a relationship, you pig."

"Don't worry about it," Owen said to Gabby, his voice purposefully light. He refused to let this idiot goad them. Gabby shifted, angling herself toward Owen in a way that pressed her front to his side, and a jolt of surprise rushed him. Since when did her body feel so good next to his? *Since you took notice of it and this jackass pointed it out.* Owen scowled at Jake. "What are you doing here?"

Jake held his hands up in an "I surrender" gesture. Owen's fist curled again and he reminded himself that it wasn't worth the effort of getting riled up. But just one punch would feel so good. He took pride in his even-keeled emotions, which definitely did not run in his family. Even his sister had engaged in a scuffle once when a girl had said some less than pleasant things about her. But not Owen. He didn't think violence was necessary. Usually.

"I had a box in storage. About this big," he said. He gestured to show an object about six inches by six inches. "Cardboard, pretty plain. I can't find it. I saw Gabby's boxes weren't down there so I wondered if maybe she grabbed it by accident. That's all, dude. I wasn't hitting on your girl."

My girl. The words warmed his insides like he'd just taken a long drink of really good coffee.

"And I told him I hadn't seen it. Have you?" Gabby asked, looking up at Owen with her still slightly slumberous eyes.

"No."

Jake shook his head like a scolded child. "Fine. If you see it, though, can you let me know?"

"Sure," Gabby said.

Jake walked away, leaving Owen and Gabby standing in her doorway. When Jake stepped onto the elevator and the doors closed, Gabby whirled on Owen, giving him a little shove. "What the hell was that?"

Owen flinched, more from surprise than pain. He captured her hand when she poked him in the chest. The residual irritation swirled in his gut, boiling over. "What was what? How many times have I told you not to be alone with him? The guy is a first-class creep."

Gabby raised her eyebrows and pushed past him into her apartment. "I was not alone with him, you dope. He knocked on my door and I answered. We were standing in the hallway. I never pegged you for a caveman."

He followed behind, leaving her door open so they could take some of her stuff to his place. He decided now wasn't the time to mention she'd been standing in the hallway wearing hardly anything. Even now, as she picked up a pile of clothes still on the hangers that were draped over the back of her couch, he could easily see the outline of her breasts. Not that he was looking.

He cleared his throat and picked up her easel, carefully, and folded the legs. *All I did was stand beside her.* "What are you talking about?"

Gabby laughed. "I'm talking about your little act out there. The she's-my-woman stomp you did, rushing from your door to mine. I think you're wasting your time staking a pretend claim on me in front of Jake. Even if we were really together, that wouldn't stop him from being a creep."

Because he had no choice, he followed her across the hall. "What do you mean staking a pretend claim?" *Why is she so mad?*

She walked into his bedroom and tossed her clothes on his bed. He cringed but set the easel against the wall and ignored the mess. He'd fix it. He wanted her in his space, so some…adjustments would be necessary.

She pulled open the double closet doors and stopped in her tracks. Her breath whooshed out and then she looked back at him. "You already cleared space for me?"

He picked up a few items and stepped around her to hang them. The job had been first on his list this morning. "Of course. I wanted to make it as easy and efficient as possible. Now what did you mean, pretend claim?"

She continued to stare and scrunched her lips together. He couldn't read her face. He hated that. It didn't happen often, but when it did, he felt like the lights went out in the room and he was enveloped in the dark.

She shrugged. "Nothing. Just, it seemed kinda…territorial, the way you rushed over and then stared him down. You looked pissed." She laughed, shaking her head.

He had been pissed, still was. He told himself it was because Jake was a dick, not because he'd felt territorial, as Gabby said. Gabby looked down at the carpet and ran her foot back and forth. Owen stepped closer. He didn't want her to be mad at him, but if it kept Jake away from her, it was worth it. But it was probably best not to tell her that.

He stopped in front of her. His thoughts flashed back to the night before, to kissing her, and the memory rocked his insides, like an unexpected wave pulling him under. The kiss had been nothing short of spectacular, but it was best for him not to think too much about it. Instead, he softened his voice and went in a different direction. "If he thinks we're a couple, it's a good thing. I won't be lucky enough to have my parents escape meeting that loser. The more people who believe we're together, the smoother things will go this week."

She looked up, and his stomach lurched. The sadness in her eyes had him reaching out to her, but stopped himself. She didn't need comfort right now. She was Gabby. The strongest woman he knew. But he didn't want to be the reason for her sadness.

She backed up slowly. "Right. Good thinking, Owen. Listen, you hang this stuff up for me, and I'll go grab a few more things. Then I have to get to work."

He grabbed her arm when she tried to step around him. "Are you sure you're okay with this?"

Gabby patted his hand before pulling out of his grasp. "Why wouldn't I be? As you said last night, I've got the better end of the deal, right? I get the apartment, a hot pretend-boyfriend, and an old-fashioned family Christmas."

Owen gave a rough laugh. "I think 'hot' is pushing it, and Christmas with my family is more likely to resemble the Griswolds than *It's a Wonderful Life*," he said.

She thinks I'm hot?

Gabby's brows arched and her wide grin tightened his stomach and chest. Hands on her hips, she chuckled. Her laugh curled around his heart and grabbed hold. "Oh my. Did you just reference two actual Christmas movies? Who are you and what have you done with my best friend?"

"I'm the guy who really appreciates you doing this, Gabs."

She stiffened. "No big deal. That's what friends are for, right?"

Before he could reply, she walked out of his room. He hung her clothes next to his, struck by a strange fluttering in his chest. He ran his hand over a dress he'd never seen her in. It was black sheer on top of colored fabric—beautiful, and he could imagine it would pair perfectly with her vibrant eyes and all that lush hair. There was something intimate about sharing closet space. He'd never done that with anyone. Vanessa had loved this apartment, probably more than she'd cared for him. But he'd asked her not to leave any of her things here. Maybe if it hadn't felt calculated on her part—leaving odds and ends in his space so she'd have a reason to pop by when he'd specifically told her he had things to do, it would've been different.

Other than with his family, he'd never shared a home, and now he'd have Gabby sharing all his space. It occurred to him that when Gabby left random things at his apartment, he didn't really care. In fact, he had what she referred to as her "Gabby-basket" tucked between the couch and the wall. He put anything she forgot or left behind in the basket.

"Gabby's different," he said, assuring himself it wasn't a big deal. She was sweet and funny and pretty damn adorable, even if she was messy. It didn't matter when it was at her place, but in his? She'd have more than a basket now, but it didn't make him squirm like he thought it might. "Because we're just friends and it's temporary." He took her easel to the living room, where he'd cleared space in front of the windows. She was doing him a favor, so he could put aside his petty need for order.

Once she left for work, he'd drag over all her boxes and her artificial tree. He'd been so happy last night, when Gabby had agreed, he'd spent most of the night thinking about her and he'd come up with a "Surprise Gabby Plan." He figured he'd score major pretend-boyfriend points when he picked her up at the end of her day and brought her home to decorate the tree. Now, he had to do what he said he would: make it easy and fun so she didn't regret saying yes.

Chapter Four

Gabby took a deep breath, irritated that her hand shook when she applied mascara. Damn Owen and his stupid be-my-girlfriend plan. She tossed the makeup on her counter, gathered up the rest of her things, and got ready to leave. Her heartbeat had gone off-kilter last night when Owen had kissed her, and it still hadn't righted itself. What the hell was she doing? *Inventing new ways to torture yourself.*

Bundled up for the walk to the bus stop, she took the elevator down to the lobby. The heels of her boots tapped along the deserted lobby tiles. She was actually looking forward to work, just to get some space from Owen and his plan. And it hadn't even started yet.

A little bit of distance was what she needed to remind herself of where she stood in his life, how great their friendship was and how poorly her last attempt at a long-term relationship worked out. Even if Owen were interested in her that way, which clearly he was not, she'd risk losing the most important person in her life. Because everything good came to an end.

As she neared the double glass doors in the bright, open foyer, one of her neighbors was letting himself in. She didn't know his name and the few times she'd ridden the elevator with him, he'd given off a vibe that suggested she shouldn't ask. He was tall—even taller than Owen, but, in Gabby's opinion, not as hot. His lips were almost always pressed into a hard, unsmiling line, and though he was attractive, he was most certainly not friendly. Generally, she steered clear. He held the door for her and she said hello.

His reply was more of a grunt, but before the door closed behind her, he said, "Hey. You're friends with Jake, the apartment manager, right?" His voice was stiff, like he kept it in reserve for only the most needed times.

It was an odd first sentence, but Gabby shrugged and went with honesty. "No. Is anyone?"

His eyes flickered with...something. Doubt? "I've seen you talking to him."

Gabby frowned and stretched out her words. "Because speaking to your neighbors is polite."

She saw the hint of a smirk and this time, she recognized the flash in his eyes: amusement.

"Is that so?"

Gabby nodded. "Mm-hmm. They might even introduce themselves." She held out her hand. "I'm Gabby."

He stared at it, one corner of his mouth twitching, like he was trying not to smile. His grasp was firm and warm. "Wyatt."

Grateful to have something to divert her thoughts, she continued. "Some people even exchange random pleasantries and get to know each other."

This time, that same corner of his mouth tipped up and she got a half smile. "Those people sound weird."

A laugh burst from her chest. Mr. Moody had a sense of humor.

"Have a good day," he said, letting the door shut. Gabby

couldn't decide whether or not he meant it. But the exchange relieved some of the stress from the morning and her mostly-sleepless night.

The bus ride was only about fifteen minutes. Usually she left for work at seven thirty, but Min, her supervisor and friend, had told her today should be the first day of Gabby's holidays. More than she had before, Gabby needed the distraction. With a new program being offered at the college, starting in January, they still had several files to get through.

The campus was small, set up so the courtyard was a hexagon, different buildings housing different programs of study. She worked in the Administration building, entering student data, helping with course registration, and other office duties. She enjoyed it, the decent hours, the environment, and the vacation time. But one day she hoped to pursue her art full time.

"I told you not to come in," Min said, shaking her head when she saw Gabby walk across the lobby and come behind the counter. Cubicles and desks were arranged around huge filing cabinets.

"Just like I told you I'd be here for a few hours to finish helping you." Plus, it gave her a chance to reset her system and convince herself that Owen's kiss hadn't been *that* great. She wouldn't get much time away from him in the following days. She'd never wanted space before, even after she'd realized she loved him. But then, she hadn't known that her gorgeous geek knew exactly how to use his lips to lull her into a kiss-coma.

Gabby stored her bag in the bottom drawer of her desk, shoved her hat and gloves in the pockets of her jacket, and then hung it and her scarf on the coat rack. A shiver wracked her from head to toe. They'd be getting more snow for sure.

Min's fingers flew over the keyboard. She'd probably been here a couple of hours already. A tiny woman, even in the four-inch heels she always wore. Her straight-cut bob was severe but suited her angular face. Her caramel colored skin was make-up free, except for the heavy dose of eyeliner she wore. She ran the office with the efficiency of a general, treated her staff with the kindness of a grandmother, and could drink them all under the table any night of the week. Gabby adored her and knew that even if a time ever came when she could give up her day job, she'd miss seeing Min.

"Okay, then. Since you're as stubborn as you are adorable, let's rock this out and close down before four," Min said. She handed Gabby a stack of folders containing student information.

Gabby rubbed her hands together, then settled them on the coffee mug Min had already placed on her desk. Yeah—she'd definitely miss her. Good thing she had no reason to worry about that pipe dream anytime soon. If she wanted the art show to be a success, she'd need to actually get something on her canvas. Frowning, she pushed the thought away. Real life came first. *Ha. Your real, pretend life of being Owen's girl.*

Gabby sighed in pleasure at the first taste of Min's coffee. "You heading home tonight for the holidays?"

Min nodded, settling at the desk across from Gabby's. "Tomorrow. My whole family will be here this year. My oldest brother and his wife are bringing the twins, so that's exciting." Min had a huge family living in Vermont, and Gabby liked trying to remember all the names and connections. Min told her she'd need a flowchart and offered to make one. Gabby couldn't imagine the whole group together. If Owen thought his family made a racket, he should listen to some of Min's stories about forty relatives with several tables pushed together end to end, talking over one another.

"Cool. Take pictures or text me, at least." One day, Gabby hoped to have a large family. While Owen preferred the quiet, she'd welcome the noise. Sometimes she got tired of her own company.

"I will. I still wish you'd come. My mom hates the thought of you being alone," Min said. *Click-clacking* filled the background as both sets of their hands tapped the keyboards, inputting transfer and registration information for new and returning students.

"I won't be alone," Gabby said. Nope. At least that much was true.

"According to Mama, being alone is better than being with a man who is missing what is right in front of his face," Min said. She shot Gabby an amused grin.

A sharp pang poked her heart. She didn't want to tell Min what she'd agreed to, especially since her friend had recently decided she could find Gabby the perfect not-Owen match. Starting tonight. One of the professors, Andrew, was hosting a holiday party and Gabby had agreed to attend with a few of their colleagues. It would be a group thing, which lessened the pressure a bit, but Andrew had wanted her to come as his date. This had been the compromise. *It might be fun.* Too bad that didn't take her mind off how right Min was.

"He's not missing anything. We're friends. Why do I have to keep telling you that?"

"Because when you fall asleep at your desk you moan his name, so it's hard to believe you," Min said.

Gabby snorted with laughter, throwing a paper clip at her friend. She didn't like keeping things from Min, or anyone, but she wasn't up to explaining how much this mattered to Owen. It was hard for people outside their friendship to understand what they meant to each other. Like a lot of people, Min wondered about the ability of men and women to maintain a long-term friendship without one person's feelings getting in the way. Gabby had wisely used Phoebe and Joey's friendship from *Friends*, but Min had come back with a *When Harry Met Sally* reference.

Even though Min liked Owen—he'd come for drinks

with them on more than one occasion and had attended a few events with the two of them—she'd have something to say about Gabby pretending to be his anything. Min wouldn't have done the same thing in her shoes, she knew that. But Min had a whole family around her, a mom who worried about her and a dad who checked in with her. Gabby didn't have that. She had Owen. And maybe a little piece of his family, since they were spending the holidays together. Was it so bad to want that? Thinking of family and moms caused a hollow ache to settle below Gabby's breasts and she rubbed the center of her chest, trying to ease a pain that would never leave.

With Christmas music playing over the speakers, Gabby told Min about Owen's parents and her holiday plans. "Owen says his whole family adores Christmas. His mom makes homemade cranberry sauce and this special herb blend for the turkey."

Min picked up her coffee cup, held it between her hands. "Yum. And why doesn't he like being with them again?"

Gabby stopped typing student numbers into the computer. "He loves them. He likes being with them. He just prefers more quiet. From what he's said, they're all very lively, animated, and busy. He's just…more reserved. He doesn't dislike Christmas, he just doesn't care for all the fuss and, according to him, they're all about the fuss. Last year, his mom invited a ton of people Owen didn't even know. It's just not his scene."

Min nodded, but Gabby worried she wasn't explaining it right. There was nothing wrong with Owen preferring more solitude than some people. It didn't bother Gabby, particularly since he didn't see her as an invasion of that need.

"Well, if you think they like to make a fuss, you really need to spend Christmas with my family. This year my mom is making a turkey, duck, and ham. Gran's making a sweet-potato mash that is out of this world. I'll try to remember and put some in the freezer to bring you a taste after the holidays."

Min continued to make Gabby's stomach growl with details of the delicious treats her family would indulge in. Gabby wasn't the greatest cook. She could follow a recipe and had never starved, but she was far from Min's capabilities. Or even Owen's. Should she try and cook something while the Burnetts were in town? Would Owen want her to? *Probably not.* She snickered to herself. *Definitely not.*

Thinking of them made her wonder about Christmas presents. She should probably get them something or at least know what Owen got them. He'd have ordered something. He worshipped online shopping and bowed down to the UPS delivery guy. They kept him from having to interact too closely with other humans. Not that he wasn't a great guy, but his work made him somewhat of a homebody, despite spending most of his time there.

"How do I choose gifts for people I don't even know?"

Min looked across the desks at Gabby. "What?" Gabby hadn't realized she'd spoken aloud.

"I need to go shopping. I have to have something for his family."

Min grabbed another file and narrowed her eyes at Gabby. "Why would Owen's friend—even *best* friend—have to purchase gifts for his family?"

Min was probing, but Gabby wasn't filling in the gaps. "Because we'll be together on the day and it feels like the right thing to do." She tried to think of what Ophelia might like, since she'd probably be the easiest of the four.

"Text Owen and ask him. Better yet, text him and tell him to pick up four lovely somethings, wrap them, and put your name on them."

Gabby laughed. She wouldn't go that far, but she would text him.

Hey. I need to get your family some gifts. Don't argue. Just give me ideas.

She waited.

When do I ever argue with you?

Gabby laughed. *Do you really want me to answer that?*

Owen's reply was quick. *No. But, really, you don't have to get anything.*

She sighed. *Owen. Answer the question. I want to make a good impression.*

Three dots hovered, telling her he was typing back. *Sweetie, there's no way you wouldn't. They're going to love you.*

Gabby stared at the term of endearment, her fingers itching to screenshot it so when it got lost in the text stream, she'd be able to pull it up easily. It was funny how something could seem playful in one moment and in the next, carve a chunk out of her heart. His casual, easy-going ability to talk about love and Gabby in the same sentence reminded her that he wasn't "in" love with her. He saw her like he did Ophelia.

When she'd crawled into bed the night before, she'd promised herself she wouldn't get so caught up in their ruse she let it feel real. She'd enjoy her chance to get her hands, and her mouth, on Owen, and then be fine when it was over. Gabby had already fallen too hard for the wrong guy before. Roger, an artist she'd met at a gallery, had ended their eight-month relationship by dumping her in the lobby of her building, loudly, with other residents, including Owen, looking on. After they'd broken up, she'd said she wouldn't make herself into something she wasn't for anyone, ever again.

Which was what made being with Owen so easy. He liked her as she was. And she wouldn't be blindsided. With Owen, she was fully aware her feelings were unrequited. It was surprising he hadn't slugged her in the arm when he'd said he loved her or spit on his palm to seal their deal.

Gabby realized Owen was still texting her and shook her

head, clearing her thoughts. He'd sent a bunch of question marks. She quickly typed back: *Never mind. I've got this. See you later.* She put her phone away so she wasn't tempted to stare at the word "sweetie."

She'd be fine. Everything would work out okay. She'd rather give being Owen's pretend girlfriend her all than miss out on the chance. Better to be broken inside from trying than whole on the outside, hiding behind her fear of rejection.

Gabby pulled the crimson shirt from her bag and quickly changed out of her plain, button-up blouse she'd arrived at work in. She wasn't really into going out on a date tonight, but she didn't want to sit around wishing she had tried. Andrew was a nice man, a successful college professor with his own home, and he was handsome. Even before Min's insistence, Gabby had decided she needed to make a serious effort to find someone to take Owen's place in her heart. Not as her friend—he'd always own that piece. But she couldn't keep lusting after him knowing he'd never feel the same.

She leaned closer to one of the mirrors in the staff bathroom and added some color to her eyes. In the low lighting, she darkened the corners of her eyes to give them a somewhat smoky appearance and tried to remember the last time she'd dressed up. It had been a while. She'd turned down date requests more than once to spend the night at Owen's eating Chinese food out of the carton and watching movies. But Min was right, she needed to give this a go. Maybe tonight would be wonderful and it would alleviate the pressure taking up full-time residence in her chest. Laughing to herself at the ridiculousness of thinking she'd get over Owen that easily, she packed up her makeup, threw her shirt in her bag, and walked out of the bathroom. Right into Owen.

Gabby squealed and dropped her bag. Owen gripped her shoulders, a startled laugh erupting from his chest. His smile was warm and soothing. "Hey. Sorry. I didn't mean to scare you."

She shook her head, trying to laugh it off. The heat of his fingertips pressing into her skin was like little spots of fire. He looked down, moved to grab her bag, but stopped, stepped back, and looked her over from head to toe. She'd stowed her flats and worn heels. Hopefully she wouldn't end up on her butt on a patch of ice.

Owen gestured to her, his eyes a little wide. "What are you…what are you wearing?"

Gabby retrieved her bag, pulling it onto her shoulder. Min had left a little while ago and security was strolling around somewhere, but the building seemed alive, despite the quiet, now that Owen was there.

"I'm wearing clothes. Seeing as you're dressed, you must be familiar with them." He followed her when she walked to her desk, where she'd left her jacket hanging over her chair.

"Ha-ha. You look good. Like, really good," he said, his voice low and his tone puzzled. Gabby put her purse down, grabbed her jacket, and faced him as she pulled it on.

"Thanks. I do dress up now and again, you know," she said, teasing. Though, when she had to, she usually went for her simple black shift dress.

He stepped closer and Gabby's breath caught. "You don't usually wear so much makeup."

Butterflies took off inside her stomach. "You think it's too much? I have a date."

Owen's mouth opened and then closed. It would have made Gabby laugh if she could find enough air to breathe. "You have a date? With *who?*"

Was she imagining the surprise in his voice? She buttoned up her coat, her fingers feeling clunky. She kept her eyes down so he couldn't see her hurt. "Yes. Imagine that, someone asked me out. No need to alert the media. It happens now and again, you know." *I just usually say no in favor of being with my idiot best friend.*

Owen's fingers tipped her chin up. Jesus, it was like his fingers were little heat pads, sending sparks through her whenever they connected with any part of her body. "Gabby. That's not what I mean. At all. I'm sorry, I just…" He dropped his hand, but he didn't back up, so Gabby was forced to continue breathing the scent of him. He ran his hands through his hair, his glasses slightly askew. "I'm just surprised. Not surprised you have a date, because you're a beautiful woman. I just…I had my own surprise planned."

If she'd been unable to breathe before, she was near to hyperventilating now. He'd just called her beautiful. And she wasn't even dreaming. Her voice came out as a squeak as her heart twisted with the happiness of hearing those words from his lips, and the sadness of knowing he meant nothing by them.

"What surprise?"

His lips pressed into a frown before he asked, "Who are you going on a date with?"

They stared at each other and she knew, from previous experience, that he could hold out longer than she could. She sighed. "Just a professor. Holiday house party. No big deal."

Owen laughed, but it sounded forced. "It's kind of a big deal. I mean, you are technically cheating on me. For pretend."

Gabby froze and her face must have registered shock, because he nudged her shoulder. *From sexy to shoulder nudging in forty seconds flat.*

"I was joking, Gabs. Though I'm kind of hoping you don't have any dates planned for the next week or so. I may like to keep my private life private, but my family knows me well enough to be sure I wouldn't go for an open relationship."

Gabby's heart ripped like paper. She didn't want to date anyone else. She wanted him to want her. She wanted this to be real.

"No. No dates. I'm all yours." *Even if you have absolutely no idea.* "You know what, I made this date before any of this. I actually forgot about it until Min texted me last night. I'm going to cancel. It's a house party, so it's not that big a deal." Though Andrew had tried to get her to agree to dinner first and she'd said no.

She expected Owen to bluster, assure her she should go on her date, and say they'd hang later. If one of his guy friends had a date he'd forgotten, Owen would have brushed off their plans. No big deal. "Yeah? You sure?" He smiled at her, and her heartbeat kicked back up.

She nodded. "I'm sure. What's my surprise?"

Owen turned and gestured for her to go first. They walked to the front of the building. Security would set the alarm later, but she locked the doors, pulling on them to be sure. The wind had picked up and the sky was denim dark.

"If I tell you, it won't be a surprise," Owen said. He opened the passenger door of his truck, but didn't close it after she was in. Instead, he stood there, looking at her. He reached out his hand and his thumb trailed down her cheek. Shivers followed. "You really do look beautiful. You sure you're okay giving up a hot date in favor of hanging out with me?"

She wanted to close her eyes and lean into his touch. "Yup." She hadn't meant to whisper.

Almost in slow motion, Owen leaned forward and put his forehead to hers. This time, she did close her eyes. Listening to the sound of their mingled breaths, she felt hyperaware of everything. His breath fanning her lips. His scent. His touch.

His lips.

If she just leaned forward a tiny bit… She opened her eyes to see Owen staring at her, the rim of his glasses resting against the bridge of her nose.

"You're the best fake girlfriend a guy could ever ask for," he whispered. He pulled back and rounded the hood of the truck. Gabby's breath *whooshed* out of her lungs and tears stung her eyes. When he climbed in and started the truck, he grinned over at her like an excited kid.

"Time to show you what a great phony boyfriend I can be," he said.

Gabby laughed, but absolutely nothing about this moment felt funny.

Chapter Five

For the second time in two days, Owen was nervous in Gabby's presence. He hated it. He was also extremely aware of how great she smelled, how sexy she looked with her eyes done up like some Hollywood movie legend. He felt like his tongue had lodged in his throat when he'd seen how she was dressed. And knowing how she tasted made it that much harder to keep his mood light and fun. They walked into their building through the downstairs parking garage in silence.

What the hell was he doing? He'd almost kissed her when she'd gotten in the car. He'd wanted to so badly, he'd clenched one hand into a fist until his fingers dug into his palm painfully. He didn't understand what was going through his head, or happening in his heart, but when she told him she had a date, he'd wanted to punch something. Twice in one day. *At least she didn't have a date with Jake.* He shuddered at the thought.

"You okay?" She leaned against the wall, closer to him in height with her heels on.

"Fine. Just hoping you like your surprise."

"I'm sure I will. Listen, do you mind if I change first? No

point in being dressed up for a night at home, right?"

She'd assured him, even as she was calling her date to cancel, that she didn't mind the change in plans. Owen had been surprised by the level of relief he felt when she said she'd bail. It was nice she didn't feel the need to dress up around him, but seeing her this way made him think he'd taken her a little for granted. Even good friends should go to some trouble for each other now and again.

"Owen?" She waved her hand in his face, smiling at him. "Hellooo?"

He laughed and grabbed her hand, meaning to keep it away from his face, but their fingers linked and he held on, lowering their hands between them as the elevator doors slid open. "No. I don't mind." They walked to her door, hand in hand, with Owen feeling something odd that he couldn't explain. Her hands were like silk. They were delicate and fit perfectly inside his own.

"Gonna need my hand back, O," Gabby said when they got to her door.

His neck warmed and he practically snatched his hand back. "Right. Sorry. Just, uh, practicing, you know?"

She looked up at him. In her heels they were practically eye level. The dark coloring around her eyes was enough to put him in a trance. He could get lost if he let himself.

Her forehead creased. "Right. Well, we can resume practicing later. I'll be over in ten, okay?"

He nodded. Even when she shut the door, he continued to stand there for a second, staring at it. He heard a slight *thud*, almost like she'd plunked herself back against the door when she'd closed it. He smiled. Nah.

All this pretending had him imagining things.

On his third turn-around from his front entryway, down the small hallway, into the living room and back, Owen realized he was pacing. His parents' impending visit was making him crazy. As was the reminder of Gabby's eyes and her lips up close. She knocked on the door just as he stopped in front of it. She didn't usually knock. He swung it open to see her dressed like she usually was: black lounge pants, no socks, and a T-shirt that read: *I'm not forgetful, I'm artsy.*

"Hey," she said, smoothing down her hair. She'd washed the makeup from her face, and though he'd liked it, she was every bit as pretty without.

"Hey, yourself. Why'd you knock?" He stepped aside, closing the door behind her.

"Wasn't sure what the surprise entailed, so it seemed safer. Why's it so dark in here?" She started moving down the hallway.

He grabbed her arm to stop her. "Wait. I want you to close your eyes."

She looked at him and her eyes twinkled. A spark of something far *too* friendly shot through him. "I'm not clumsy enough for you?"

He laughed, pushed down the errant spark of interest, and turned her back toward the living room, covering her eyes with one hand and placing the other on her shoulder. As he guided her forward, he heard her inhale.

"Something smells yummy. Mm. I'm starving," she said.

He chuckled. "I figured you would be. Seeing as you're awake and all."

Her hand flailed out to swat him, smacking him on the lower abdomen, dangerously close to where the spark had been. She giggled and Owen focused on not walking her into a wall.

When they reached the doorway of the great room that encompassed the living area, office area, and kitchen, he stopped them.

"I, um…borrowed a few of your things. I hope you don't mind," he said.

"Okay." That simple. No questions, no balking. What was hers was his. God, he hoped he was as good a friend to her as she was to him. He'd have to start making sure of it.

"Do I smell egg rolls?" she asked, her chin jutting upward. She sniffed.

Owen laughed, the tension easing out of his shoulders, and he withdrew his hands, stepping out from behind her so he could see her face. She looked around, her mouth slightly open. He'd kind of copied what he'd seen her do in her place. He'd put the decorative fir garland along the fireplace mantel, tucking it behind a small nativity scene that he knew had belonged to her parents. Stocking hangers—one ceramic Santa Claus and one goofy-looking snowman—sat at either end, stockings dangling from their hooks. The floor-to-ceiling windows showcased the hanging stars he'd found in one of her boxes. Eight large stars hung down, twinkling against the glass and the black sky beyond. On the bar-eating area that separated the kitchen from the living area, he'd set out a bunch of appetizers—Gabby loved bite-sized food.

But it was when she turned and saw the tree taking up the corner of the room that he knew he'd done well.

Her hands rose slowly to her mouth. He hadn't decorated it, just put the lights on and made sure they worked. They danced on and off. Last year, Gabby set everything up herself and had, in passing, mentioned it was kind of a lonely job but she loved how it transformed everything. This year, he wanted to share it with her. Shoving both hands in his pockets, Owen rocked back and forth on the balls of his feet, watching her.

Her eyes were glassy when they met his. "You did all this? I can't believe you did all this *for me*. It's amazing and beautiful. You're going to decorate the tree with me? I can't even believe I didn't have it up yet and now I'm so glad I waited, well, got sidetracked and busy, really, but same thing, right?" She waved her hands and gave a watery laugh.

And then she stepped into him, her arms slipping around his waist. She put her head against his chest and gave a deep sigh. Of happiness, he hoped. Owen was worried that the shock coursing through him was more from the feel of her body pressed so tightly to his rather than her show of gratitude. His arms immediately wrapped around her and he rubbed his hands up and down her back.

"It's perfect, Owen. Absolutely perfect."

Still holding her, the sense of how well her body fit against his tugging at the strings of worry in the back of his head, he held tighter. "Good enough to make up for you canceling a date?"

She leaned back so they were looking at each other, their arms still wrapped around each other. Owen's chest felt tight. Maybe he was allergic to fake trees. What else could account for the shortness of breath he felt?

"There is nowhere I'd rather be," Gabby said. They held each other's gaze and when his brain screamed to step back before he did something he shouldn't, her hands moved to his face. He'd never had a woman cradle his face in her hands quite like this, with a look of absolute adoration. It was mesmerizing. Gabby was mesmerizing. Somehow he'd missed that.

She went up on tiptoe, bringing their faces closer, and he heard her breath hitch. "Earlier you mentioned practicing," she said.

Owen's heart beat heavy in his ears. "Yeah?"

"We should probably do more of that." Her voice was a whisper but he had no trouble hearing her, even with his pulse pounding.

"Uh. I guess we should," he said.

"We want it to feel natural, or at least look natural," she said.

He nodded because speaking had become difficult. Like she was waiting to see if he'd pull away, Gabby moved her face, her mouth, closer to his one millimeter at a time. His fingers clenched the fabric of her shirt. How could seconds take so long to pass? When her mouth finally touched his, he felt like he'd been waiting a lifetime. Thinking stopped as her lips brushed against his, teasingly. When she sighed, her body sinking into his, his brain shut down. His hands moved up, over her graceful back and into her hair. She pressed impossibly closer, but her lips pulled away so they hovered near his. When her tongue traced lightly along his bottom lip, he all but jumped back away from her, his breath sawing in and out like he'd climbed a mountain. He saw the look of hurt on her face, saw the glow in her eyes dim.

"Sorry," she whispered.

Damn it. "No. Don't be sorry." He laughed too loud. Hell, he should be sorry. For something. He just didn't know what. He moved to the counter and started loading a couple of plates with food. "We need to practice, so no big deal. Though we probably don't need to make out in front of my family. Maybe just stick to some light kissing, some hand holding." And even that felt like it might push him over an edge he hadn't even realized existed.

"Right. Sounds good. Got carried away. Christmas does that to me."

It'd never done it to him before, but right now he had to fight the urge to pull her closer again. He was just caught up in her enthusiasm. Right? He passed her a plate, smiling so wide his cheeks ached. "Anyway, I'm glad you like your surprise. Let's eat and then we'll decorate the tree."

The happiness he'd seen didn't come back into her gaze, but she smiled and sat on the couch. Worried he'd hurt her, which he never wanted to do, he sat close so their thighs were touching. He'd meant it to be natural, but she definitely noticed. Her eyes widened and she glanced down, then picked up an egg roll and took a huge bite. He tried to pretend the feel of her leg against his was nothing unusual. Just another night, hanging out with Gabby, eating good food. In the romantic Christmas lighting, about to decorate a tree, something that meant a lot to her.

After sharing a mind-altering kiss.

While pretending they were a couple.

Right. Perfectly normal.

He just hoped that after all this was over, everything would go back to the way it was before. Before he'd crossed a line he now wondered if he could ever uncross.

Chapter Six

Setting her paintbrush down, Gabby's heart beat heavily as she stared at the tornado of colors rioting off the canvas, swirling into each other. Losing herself in her work made her feel like she'd fallen into another world, emerging like Alice at the bottom of the rabbit hole. And maybe she had. Pretending to move into Owen's house — creating in his space — gave her the same jolt she thought Alice might have felt when she tumbled into Wonderland.

Gabby blinked and stretched, shaking out her arms. Feeling like she was indeed in her own version of a fairy tale, she eyed her work. She was happy with what she'd produced in the last hour and a bit. It had promise, and she felt certain it would end better than the charade with Owen. Her stomach growled loudly and she glanced at the clock. *Owen will be back soon enough.* He'd gone to get groceries and stock up on a few things.

After decorating the tree last night, they'd watched *National Lampoon's Christmas Vacation* together. As "practice," Owen had put his arm around her shoulders and she'd nestled into him. Good thing she'd already seen the movie because she was too aware of their every breath and the feeling of being curled up against him on the couch. She'd left immediately after the movie and had spent most of the night staring at her ceiling thinking about how good it felt to cuddle into Owen. Being tucked into his side with the lights dim and the tree aglow had felt natural and romantic. She'd lost sleep telling herself not to forget it wasn't real.

Now, she rolled her shoulders to relieve the stiffness that had settled there. She needed a break and to stretch her legs. Leaving her brush on her work station, she eyed the boxes stacked neatly by the door, out of the way. She'd take them down to storage. If it was her place—or she wasn't feeling like she needed to do something—she'd have left them. She cleaned up her brushes first and wiped down the sink after washing them. This morning, she'd been extra careful not to leave crumbs or dishes on the counter. It wasn't like he would say anything, but it felt weird being in someone else's home. *His* home. Surrounded by his things and very aware of her own belongings mingling in with his. Already the space was more cluttered than usual and Gabby couldn't help thinking if they really lived together, she'd drive him crazy. They might be pretending, and even though she was doing Owen a favor, she knew having things clutter his space—like the boxes—would make him crazy.

He'd just take them down when he got home, and since he was grabbing food, it only seemed fair to get them out of the way. She grabbed the dolly that typically stayed in the storage room and piled her boxes on it. As she waited for the elevator and made her way to the basement, she thought about her particular place in Owen's life.

When they'd met, she'd been with Roger and he'd been with Vanessa. They'd been strangers and she never would have predicted the amount of space he'd end up taking over in her heart. They'd arrived within minutes of each other, she alone and Owen with Boston Barbie, to put deposits on units. Jake had informed them there were two units available. One was slightly more expensive but had more to offer.

Obviously, both of them wanted the larger unit with its bonus features. Gabby had all but salivated when she'd seen the tall windows, the gleaming wood floors, granite kitchen counters, and the wide-open space. She remembered Vanessa pushing Owen to fight for it when he'd seemed willing to bow out. Gabby's heart had sunk when she'd lost the coin toss, but she'd certainly faced worse losses in her life and was able to take it in stride. It was certainly easier to take than Vanessa's tacky victory whoop and the smacking kiss she'd given Owen, as if she'd just won a prize. Owen had flushed red and looked oddly embarrassed by his girlfriend's display.

Because they'd both been with other people, they shared only casual greetings for the first several months. They chatted at the mailbox and he'd made her laugh a few times in the elevator. But when Roger had broken up with her loudly in the lobby of the building like he was giving the performance of his life, Owen had shown up later that night with a large pizza.

She'd kept her head down while Roger made a fool of her and hadn't been aware which of her neighbors were treated to the spectacle. Humiliation had formed a barrier around her and she couldn't see outside it, but she heard every word. So did anyone within fifty feet as Roger listed Gabby's faults. He'd claimed her tendency to run late proved she never put him first, she didn't support him enough as an artist and was selfishly consumed with her own work, she was needy and holding him back from success. She'd known, even at the time, he was reeling over rejection from a gallery who'd been considering his work. But his words had dug into Gabby's confidence. She couldn't be something she wasn't and she clearly wasn't what Roger wanted. Even now, embarrassment swamped her, though these days she was more upset she'd let him treat her like that. If she hadn't been so floored, so utterly stunned at being publically dumped by a man she thought loved her, perhaps she'd have done more than stand there.

Gabby steadied the dolly, one hand on the boxes, and leaned to push open the storage door. She squealed when it was pulled open before she even touched it. She jarred backward but caught herself.

"Oh, hey Gabby," Jake said, holding the door.

Her lungs stopped seizing. "You scared the heck out of me!"

"Sorry. You got that?"

She nodded, her heart still thumping madly. Everyone in the building was assigned an area of shelving in the massive storage room. It was well organized and neat, considering there were eighteen units. Each section was numbered by apartment and separated by planks. It reminded Gabby of a giant version of mail slots. The space was long enough for her Christmas tree box to slide in on its side and tall enough to stack a couple of copy-paper boxes. More than enough for her. She loaded her boxes onto her shelf. She could feel Jake's eyes on her and tried to ignore the irritation that naturally came with being anywhere near him.

"Did you find your stuff?" Gabby pushed the hair out of her eyes and set the dolly in the corner of the room.

Still holding the door, Jake's mouth tightened. When he shook his head, strands of hair swept over his forehead. "No. You know, everyone seems real nice, but maybe we need some security cameras down here. We're putting a lot of trust in people we don't really know."

Gabby agreed, though she wasn't about to tell him it was him she didn't fully trust. The cameras weren't a bad idea. *Maybe then the owner could see what a slacker he's hired.*

"Maybe bring it up at the next tenants' meeting. It's got to be about time for one of those," Gabby suggested.

He looked back at the door as it shut, his expression dark. "Yeah, maybe. That's not a bad idea. Maybe I should call one of those. Put some pressure on everyone in person."

Gabby rolled her eyes. Not exactly what she meant. "What was in it, again?"

His eyes shifted away from her face. "Just some stuff I was storing for a friend. I promised I'd take care of it and now it's gone. But I'll find it. You know what, maybe we need a sign-in or something. Then I'd know who was in here." His hands moved when he talked, like they were animating his words.

"You said it wasn't big?"

Jake's eyebrows scrunched together until they were almost touching. "No. Why?"

Gabby shrugged. "Just wondered why you didn't keep it in your place. I always put stuff down here that I'm not going to need for a long time."

"Yeah, well, I thought it was safe. How was I supposed to know someone would steal from me?"

Gabby shrugged. Not much she could say. She found it hard to believe anyone would steal from Jake or any of the other tenants. The people she'd met were nice, and a few of them, like Owen, had become her friends.

Jake was silent as they rode the elevator back to the lobby, which suited Gabby fine. Wishing she'd brought her phone, she wondered what time it was. When the silver doors slid open, Jake cut in front of her and headed toward his office. Gabby took a side hallway that led to a wall of mailboxes.

Not that she received much other than bills and junk mail, but she liked to check every few days or so. Leaning closer, she saw the grey metal door of her box looked bent in the corner. *What the?* She fingered the corner of the metal, careful not to cut herself. Checking a few of the others, she noted hers wasn't the only one. It was almost like someone had pried something into the corners, like a letter opener or a flat screwdriver.

When had she last checked her mail? The damage had to be recent; she couldn't have missed this. Which meant someone had tried to get to her mail, but why? The mailman had a key for the building, but in the years she'd been here, there had never been a problem. Frowning, she opened her box with no difficulty—the damage didn't affect it—and grabbed her handful of bills and junk flyers. They needed a recycling bin in the tiny room to get rid of the useless flyers. Still, she read the one that offered fifty percent off carpet cleaning as she walked back toward the lobby. She crumpled it when she remembered she wouldn't need to worry about carpets in her new place. Heading for Jake's office to tell him about the mailboxes, she heard commotion and several people talking over one another.

"Listen, he isn't home so I can't let you guys in. Wait, there's his girlfriend. Gabby. C'mere," Jake called. Cold air tunneled through the open door. Three women and a man stood just outside the doors, bundled in winter coats, each pulling a suitcase. Her stomach felt like a bouncy castle.

Owen wasn't back yet and his family was early. He hadn't expected them until tomorrow at the earliest. *He said tomorrow.*

"Gabby. Get in here, doll," Jake said, waving her over.

She glared at him quickly before hurrying over. Gabby shivered even as Jake let the door close behind them. *Of course I'm cold.* She was still wearing yoga pants, a tank top, and fuzzy slipper socks. Her hair was a mess and she most likely had paint somewhere on her face. Definitely on her arms. And now she was meeting the family of the only person who really mattered to her. Like this. Whether she liked it or not.

She recognized his parents and sister from photographs in his apartment. The other woman shared the same nose and eyes as his mother. Patty. His aunt Patty.

"Um, hi. You're Owen's family. I'm Gabriella. Owen's…g-girlfriend." Her cheeks heated at the stammer in her voice. *Act natural.*

"Oh, I'm so happy to meet his Gabby. I'm Beth, his mom. That's his dad, Leo, our daughter, Ophelia—we call her Lia—and that's my sister, Patty." Beth's face was red from the wind, but warm and welcoming as she spoke animatedly. Without warning, she gripped Gabby's shoulders and pulled her into a freezing hug. Gabby's mind was still stuck on being called *his.* Twice in two days that had happened. Her heart circuits might overload.

"For goodness sakes, Beth, let the girl go. She might not even be a hugger," Owen's dad said, a wide smile on his face. Tall like Owen, he looked like a filled-out version of his son. Owen had his mother's dark hair and his father's eyes. Beth let her go and beamed at her, gloved hands clasped to the front of her chest.

"I am," Gabby said. They stared at her blankly. "A hugger. I like to hug." She wanted to sink into the floor and disappear. She sounded like the snowman from that Disney movie. She silently begged herself to do better. *What is wrong with you? You've met people before! You like people. You're good with people.*

"Well then, let me have one," Leo said, his voice booming in the open lobby. He wrapped his arms around her and said, "Nice to meet you, Gabby. Where's that boy of mine?"

"He's uh—at the store. Getting food. Groceries. To eat. We can…go upstairs," Gabby said. Maybe by the time he got back, her ability to speak in full sentences would return. She shook Ophelia's hand. Hair the same color as Owen's was tucked back in a ponytail. She didn't lean in for a hug but smiled. "We're harmless, I promise," Ophelia said, grinning

Gabby's chest loosened just in time to get a third hug, this time from Aunt Patty. The ride up in the elevator was crowded and noisy. They talked over one another, finished each other's sentences, and fawned over Gabby. *Isn't she pretty? Isn't she cute? Owen has chosen well. About time he's come to his senses.* Gabby wondered if the back of her neck could get any warmer. Owen had obviously told them about her before, just not as his girlfriend.

She let them into the apartment and listened to their compliments on the space, already loving the vibrant, lively way they talked over and around and with each other. Though their admiration for the apartment gave her a twinge of guilt for accepting the trade. It really was a great place. But as Owen had said, he didn't love it like she did and he'd probably still spend most of his time there. Until he found a real girlfriend. She couldn't stop reminding herself of that important fact. Because if she forgot, it would hurt even worse when they went back to normal.

"What do you do, Gabby?" Beth pulled off her bulky gray jacket, her scarf, mittens, and her hat. She tossed them on Owen's couch. Ophelia and Leo followed suit. Only Aunt Patty hung things, but even then, she hung them on the kitchen chairs. Gabby couldn't help but stare, her lips twitching with the urge to smile. Clearly, Owen was the only one in his family with a need for clean. Suitcases made a labyrinth in the entry way with boots strewn about, leaving water marks on the floor. Owen was going to go into spasms.

She grabbed some hangers from the hall closet as she spoke. "I'm a receptionist at the New England Institute for Art four days a week. And an artist. Though only one of those has a steady paycheck," she said.

Leo laughed. "Our Lia knows what that's like, don't you, honey?"

There was no judgment on her dad's part and no embarrassment on Ophelia's. "Amen. I'm just happy when one of the commercials I've done starts getting replayed. Royalties can be a life saver," she said.

Gabby didn't know what to do once she'd hung their clothes. She tugged their suitcases against the wall while his parents settled in on the couch and Patty and Ophelia warmed themselves by the fire, which they'd located the switch for immediately. From the corner of her eye, Gabby saw Ophelia give her aunt's hand a squeeze.

"Just leave that stuff, dear," Beth said.

Right. Owen would love that. He wouldn't even be able to open the door if she didn't move the boots.

"It's okay. I'll just tuck things out of the way," Gabby replied with an "I'm-so-breezy" arm wave.

Did Owen want his parents' stuff in his room? Her stomach lurched. She froze just as she stepped in a small puddle growing bigger from a chunk of ice. Where would *she* sleep? They hadn't discussed it. She hadn't even thought of it. How had she not thought about *that*? They were supposed to have the whole night to talk and hang out and deal with the reality of pretending in front of an audience tomorrow.

"I think we've overwhelmed her," Aunt Patty said, opening cupboards and searching through them.

Gabby waved her hands and spoke quickly. Her throat was dry as the words scratched their way to the surface. "No. No, not at all." Just because she didn't have a family and even when she did, they'd been far more reserved than this lot, didn't mean she was unable to make them feel comfortable. At home. "Can I help you find something, Patty?"

"I need to warm my bones. I'm sure Owen has some tea," she answered.

That she could do. "Of course. Let me get that for you, please." Patty gave a ghost of a smile and Gabby wondered how long she'd been married and what led to the divorce. None of her business, of course, but she couldn't help but be curious. She wondered if Christmas was harder than other times, like it was for Gabby. Holidays had a way of reminding people they were alone.

"Oh, wow. Did you paint this, Gabby?" Ophelia was standing in front of Gabby's unfinished painting. "Mom, look at this."

Gabby wasn't used to showing her work in a partially finished state. Other than Owen, no one saw it before it was completed. And him only because he came and went as he pleased. She'd planned to cover the canvas or at least move it before they'd arrived. *Tomorrow.* She ducked her head but reminded herself she was asked to participate in a very prestigious showing. There would be strangers constantly looking at and judging her work, so this was a good trial run.

"I did. It's the first in a group of five for a show I'm participating in at the Klein Gallery. That's a local gallery here in Boston."

"It's beautiful. I love the color and the lines," Ophelia said.

Leo sank farther into the couch and put his feet up on the reclaimed-wood coffee table that Owen loved. Beth wandered over to the painting, saying nothing at first. Gabby felt frozen, glued to the spot in Owen's kitchen.

"Lia's right. It's just lovely. Is that a heart in the center of a storm?" Beth looked over at Gabby, a quiet, assessing smile in her eyes. *Perceptive.* Owen's mom tucked a strand of her short hair behind her ear and Gabby couldn't help but notice her resemblance to Owen.

Patty pulled mugs out from the cupboard and opened the fridge, rooting around. It was like watching a tennis match. Gabby's eyes swung from one family member to the next. Leo clicked on the TV.

Her eyes went back to Beth. "It is," she said, impressed the woman had recognized the faint outline at the center of all the color. She'd nestled the shape in a storm of color before she was done so it wouldn't be so easy to recognize.

"Owen never mentioned your work, but he's said plenty about you. While you were friends, of course. I was certainly surprised to hear you two had taken the next step. All the time I'd ask him, are you sure she's just a friend? How can she be just a friend? I can't believe it took you two this long to end up together," Beth said. Leo chuckled and rolled his eyes, but Beth kept talking. "I was always asking, don't you want to be more than friends? And he'd say, Mom, really, we're just friends, nothing else. I knew there was more. I could *feel* it. But of course, a boy doesn't tell his mother everything."

"Thank God for that kindness," Patty said behind her as she filled the kettle.

"Mom, breathe. Maybe let Gabby breathe," Ophelia said, shaking her head with a smile.

Gabby smiled so wide her cheeks hurt, unsure of what to say.

Beth put her hands on her hips. "What'd I do? I'm just excited. And to think, he probably wouldn't have told us a thing if we hadn't decided enough was enough. We live a train ride away and he can't come home for Christmas? The holidays are for family."

Gabby's heart pinched, but no one noticed her wince. Ophelia put an arm around her mother and led her back to the fireplace. "Gee, I wonder why Owen doesn't want to tell you everything."

"Though I can see why he wouldn't want to leave you, Gabby. Especially on your own." In a hushed tone, Beth leaned closer and continued. "Owen said you have no family, is that right, dear?"

Gabby laughed in part because the whole situation was

funny but also because, what else could she do? She was saved from having to answer Beth's question when the door opened.

It closed and Owen's voice called out. "Gabs? I'm back. Sorry it took so long. Hey, I was thinking, we should probably talk about sleeping arrang…" Owen's voice trailed off and Gabby could picture him taking in the suitcases and the boots as he neatly stored his own. When he appeared in the doorway that separated the living room-kitchen area from the entryway, he stopped, several bags in each hand and stared, open mouthed.

Gabby nearly sagged with relief. "Guess who's early?" Their eyes locked and she wasn't sure if the look he gave was panic or pleasant surprise.

Perhaps a good dose of both.

Chapter Seven

Owen tightened his grip on the bags he was holding. Gabby stood in the middle of the lovable—in small doses—chaos that was his family. Her eyes were wider than normal and maybe a little wary. He didn't know whether to laugh or swear. He didn't have a chance to do either before his parents were on him.

His dad took the bags after giving him several hard slaps on the back. Owen swore he felt his bones move.

"Good to see you, son. About time," his dad said, his booming voice bouncing off the walls. His mother's hug was all consuming. She rocked back and forth, her arms nearly strangling him. It was like he'd been overseas rather than a few hours away. He'd been home once since last Christmas when he went to see one of their theater productions. She acted like it had been a lifetime.

Owen tried to pull out of his mom's clutches. "Mom. Okay." He laughed. "Let go, you're choking me."

"I missed you. I wouldn't have to hug you so hard if I didn't miss you so much."

Owen laughed and squeezed her back, feeling instantly horrible at the hint of tears he heard in her tone. He kissed her cheek. "I missed you, too." Maybe he needed to add being a better son along with being a better friend to his to-do list.

As soon as she let him go, Ophelia was there and then Aunt Patty. Patty looked happy enough, though her tired eyes suggested she wasn't getting much sleep. Owen couldn't imagine going through the break-up of a nearly four-decade marriage. His dad came back from the kitchen, handing Owen a beer. Owen took it, figuring it couldn't hurt.

"You never told us Gabby was so pretty," his mother said. Owen's eyes found Gabby, leaning against one of the stools he had at the breakfast bar. Her cheeks were pink. He hadn't ever mentioned it, he supposed. It wasn't the first thing that came to mind when he spoke of her or thought of her. Or it *hadn't* been. Now, he couldn't stop thinking about it; how pretty she looked in the quiet light of the Christmas tree or when she was focused on her art. How she'd snuggled into his side last night while he'd had to hold his breath and think too hard about Chevy Chase just to make sure his body didn't cross out of any "friend zone," even in his mind. Never a problem before, but it certainly had been last night.

Show time. He walked over and gave her a small kiss on the cheek, whispering in her ear, "You okay?" and felt her nod. Of course she was. Gabby was great in a crowd. Owen was the one who didn't like feeling hemmed in.

"I grabbed food. You guys must be hungry. We didn't expect you until tomorrow," Owen said. Moving into the kitchen, he opened one of the grocery bags and started unloading purchases. Gabby followed him and did the same. She stood close enough that their arms brushed when they moved. He was too aware of her now and it was jumbling his thoughts.

His mother inserted herself between them and pushed

their hands aside. "Never mind feeding us. We weren't expecting you to do that. I'll cook. Let me see what you've got here. You two go sit down and visit." She shooed them, actually waved her hands at them to get them to leave.

His dad laughed and lifted his beer. "Don't argue with her, son. Get over here."

"Yes, please. Let them interrogate someone else for a change." Ophelia sat down on the raised, stone hearth of the fireplace. She grinned and wound her hair up on top of her head in that strange way women did. He'd missed seeing his sister but texted with her on a regular basis. His mother wouldn't miss him so much if she'd let them teach her how to text. Maybe he'd insist on it over the next few days.

Owen took Gabby's hand, squeezing it, and led them over to the love seat. They sat hip to hip, as they had in the past, but he kept his fingers laced with hers. It felt easier than it had last night. More natural. *Maybe because you can't think about her body while your family is sitting right here. Only now you're thinking about her body. What the hell, man?* Patty was sipping tea in the kitchen and arguing with his mom's choices on what to cook. Owen felt like he should be prepping the meal for his company but knew his mother wanted to cook for her whole family. Besides, he wanted to stick close to Gabby. She wasn't used to big families and though there were only four of them visiting, they had the personalities for ten.

"So Gabby, tell us more about your art show," Ophelia said, stretching out her long legs.

Owen glanced at her with a smile. "You told them about your show?" She was typically shy about her work and adorably superstitious of jinxing herself by talking about success before it happened. He had far more faith in her inevitable success than she had for herself.

Gabby pointed to her canvas. "I didn't get a chance to cover it."

Owen got up from the couch, stepped over his sister, and moved closer to the painting. He never understood where her ideas came from. She'd start with nothing and by the time she was finished, she told a story, one layer at a time. She had paintings and sketches he stared at endlessly, always seeing something new, always feeling something new. This was the same canvas she'd started the other night before he'd interrupted her. More color had been added, more depth with the addition of thick, painted brushstrokes. She'd gotten quite a bit done while he'd been gone. She had to be nervous about his family having seen it, but when he looked back at her, it was him she was watching, not his sister or parents.

His stomach did one small flip when their eyes met. Looking away, ignoring the sensation, he took in her canvas and pride swamped him. "It's going to be incredible, Gabs. I love the colors. Is there symbolism in the fact that this outline looks like a heart at the center of chaos?" He'd been unsure, but he saw by the quick intake of breath and the way she darted her eyes down to the floor, then back up, that he was right. Why would it bother her that he'd understood? Ignoring the feel of his family's attentive stares—he'd never had a significant other be part of a family occasion—he walked back to the couch, ran a hand down Gabby's hair. Now that he knew how soft it was, he had a hard time *not* touching it.

"It's beautiful, Gabby. Like you." He kissed her cheek as he sat beside her again, wondering if he'd ever told her she was pretty. He must have. She used to stop by his apartment and ask for an opinion on her date outfits. None of them had rivaled what she'd worn last night, but surely he'd said she looked gorgeous or beautiful. Her hand on his thigh arrested his train of thought. The subtle warmth of her palm on his leg was all he could feel, and he did his own fast intake of air. Their eyes locked.

"You're biased."

Obviously, he hadn't told her enough. He'd change that from now on. Covering her hand, he wondered if, going forward, everything would change. No. He wouldn't let this week of pretending affect their friendship. He relied on it too much. Neither of their track records in terms of long-term relationships were especially good. If they crossed that line, for real, he'd be risking a connection with someone who made him laugh, who understood him, who he truly enjoyed. Romance ended. Friendship—*their* friendship—was forever.

It didn't matter that he knew how her lips felt against his or how she tasted. Or that she made a small sound in the back of her throat when his hands moved up her body. That wouldn't change anything. What they had was too special to be wrecked by some slight pull of unexpected attraction. *Okay, strong pull. At the moment, Herculean pull. Stop it.*

The smell of garlic filled the air, reminding him how hungry he was and that his family was right here, in his house. The sizzling sound coming from the kitchen and his mom's laughter at something Patty said felt homey. It felt better than he'd thought it would and he wondered why he'd waited so long—held back from welcoming his family into his home.

Ophelia asked if he had any cards, and while his mom and dad regaled them with stories of theater students, they taught Gabby how to play Hearts.

Ophelia shuffled the deck with the speed of a Vegas dealer she'd played on a show once.

Gabby shook her head in wonder. "So it's called Hearts but you don't want to pick them up?"

"I should have taught you this sooner. Lia is a shark," Owen said.

His sister stuck her tongue out at him. "And Owen is a sore loser."

Gabby laughed, the sound light and, oddly enough, sexy. She lowered herself onto the floor, crossing her legs and getting comfortable as they told her the basic rules. He'd forgotten how much he loved sitting around playing cards. Other than poker with Brady and a couple of Brady's mechanic friends, Owen hadn't played in a long while. He'd spent many nights getting his butt kicked by Lia. It had never occurred to him to ask Gabby if she wanted to play.

"I'm well aware of the sore loser part," Gabby said after glancing at her cards.

"What?" Owen looked up and scowled at Gabby's grin.

"He's been like that since he was a toddler," his mom called from the kitchen. Patty agreed loudly enough for them all to hear.

Had he just been thinking it was nice to have them here? "When am I a sore loser?" He arched an eyebrow, daring Gabby to give an example.

She shared a look with Ophelia. "Um, any time we play one of your video games?"

"Because you win by luck, not skill," he said. Which actually did piss him off. But mostly because, if he was a sore loser, Gabby was a worse winner. The few times she managed to beat him, she'd toss the controller like she was dropping the mic. Then she performed some sort of ridiculous victory dance while he tried to get her to go one more round.

"You're making their case for them, Owen," his dad said.

Outnumbered, he pointed a finger at Gabby. "Should I tell them how you celebrate a win?" Her cheeks flushed pink from the truth of his words, but he was interrupted before he could tease her about it.

"Owen and Lia, stop arguing and come set the table," his mother called.

Owen let out a growl of frustration. "Mom! What are we? Eight?" Okay, maybe he was a sore loser. Gabby's smirk didn't settle the irritation brewing under his skin.

"If you were eight, I'd give you a good swat for that tone," his mom replied.

Standing, he threw his hands up when the others, including Gabby, laughed. One evening with them and he was as dramatic as they were.

"I'll help, too," Gabby said. She held out a hand to him, and when he pulled her up to standing, her body brushed up against his. He put his hand on her waist, meaning to steady her or stop her, or maybe just touch her. Whatever reason he'd had vanished, along with any irritation. For a second, it was just his hand on her nicely rounded hip, touching bare skin where her tank top slid up a little. She bit her lip, looking at him through lowered lashes. He stared at her, caught in the easy way she smiled at him and touched his shoulder.

"Which means you have to move out of my way, O," she said. Her tone was so amused that he wanted to kick himself. He'd thought, for a second, she felt the same heat surround them when they touched. But she looked at him with such indulgence, he figured he imagined it. *Because it's not real, you idiot. She's doing exactly what you asked and you're turning it into something else.*

They made it through dinner with a minimum of "let's embarrass the hell out of Owen" stories. He kicked his sister once under the table, which his mother actually scolded him for.

Ophelia laughed even as she played up the injury. "As if you've never told humiliating stories in front of my boyfriends."

"That's different," Owen griped, twirling the spaghetti around his fork. "Your boyfriends were losers."

"Hey," Lia said.

His mom set down her drink sharply. "Do you need to leave the table, Owen?"

"Jesus, Mom," Owen said, hanging his head.

Everyone chuckled, but Gabby squeezed his hand under

the table and that made the rest not matter.

"I don't scare easy. If I haven't run yet, I probably won't," Gabby said, quietly so only he could hear her. Which was strange, since it was the perfect pretend girlfriend thing to say.

"Beth," she continued, "this pasta sauce is delicious. I've eaten in Italian restaurants that aren't as good." He almost kissed her for so easily diverting his family's attention.

His mom sat up straighter, giving Gabby a toothy smile. "Aren't you the sweetest thing? Thank you, honey. Do you like to cook?"

Owen snorted and earned a pinch from Gabby. "What?" he asked as he removed her fingers from his leg. "You don't like to cook. You like to be fed. Most days, by the time I see you, you haven't even remembered to eat."

"That's not good. It's not healthy," his mom said, passing more biscuits down to Gabby.

She took them and scowled at Owen. "I eat. It's only when I'm caught up in something that I forget. Owen makes a good sauce, but yours is definitely better."

Owen swore she would have stuck her tongue out at him if no one had been looking. He squeezed her hand. "Maybe *she'll* make it for you at midnight when you haven't eaten all day."

Ophelia sighed. "That's so sweet. You do that? Who would have thought my uptight little brother could be so romantic?"

Romantic? He'd brought Gabby meals at all hours on the weekends. Sometimes she forgot to take care of herself when she was deep in a project. Not that she couldn't, but he liked checking on her, seeing her progress and making sure she was doing fine. He liked just being with her, but he hadn't intended those gestures to be romantic. Did Gabby think they were romantic? Had she thought he was hitting on her? *Had* he been, without even realizing it? Panic fluttered tiny wings in his chest.

Was there a chance they'd always been headed here? Was there any possibility that if they did explore this, for real, it would work? Why hadn't he wondered before? Thinking about it now made him feel like there was a boot on his lungs, blocking his airway.

"So Gabby, what does your family do over the holidays?" Patty asked.

Owen froze, his eyes darting to Gabby. He'd shared with his parents and sister that Gabby didn't have a family, but no one had mentioned it to his aunt.

Before he could fill in the silence, Gabby spoke. Because he knew her so well, he knew every word tore at her insides. "I don't have a family. My parents died when I was a teen. A car crash. Both of my parents were only children. I lived with my mother's parents for a few years after the accident, but they died when I was twenty-one. My father's parents passed away when I was little."

Patty gave a small gasp. "Oh, honey. I'm so sorry. That's so much loss at such a young age. Though I don't know that loss at a later age is any easier."

"I'm sorry, Gabby," Ophelia said softly.

"We all are, sweetheart," Leo said, reaching over to squeeze Gabby's hand.

"You can just consider us your family now," Beth added.

Gabby's lips firmed into a tight line and she nodded, her eyes catching Owen's. He hated the wetness he saw. Reaching under the table, he linked their fingers again.

"Thank you, everyone. It was a long time ago."

But Owen knew it would never be long enough for her to heal or put her guilt behind her. He was grateful when Patty enthusiastically shifted the topic.

"We need to do a bit of Christmas shopping," Patty said.

Owen bit back his groan when his mom and Ophelia jumped on board.

His mother pushed her plate forward. "I've been looking online the last few days," she started.

"Scary words," Ophelia said. Owen laughed and their mom gave them a mock frown.

"There are a bunch of festive activities going on. Tree trimmings at a park not too far from here, carol singing in different neighborhoods, a wrap party—that's with a 'w,'" Mom said, pausing for them to give an obligatory laugh. Owen rolled his eyes, but she continued. "Have you been to any of them, yet? I was thinking we could choose a couple to do tomorrow."

Owen's brain hurt, but he said nothing. His dad caught his eye and grinned. "Learn to go along with it, son. We'll all come. Right, Gabby?"

"You will join us tomorrow, right, dear? We'll have lunch and shop and make a day of it," Beth said.

Owen and his father finished the last of their meals and both of them stood to clear their plates.

Gabby finished off half a biscuit and wiped her hands on her napkin. She glanced at Owen, a reassuring smile on her lips. "Absolutely. That sounds like fun."

Her eyes sparkled. He had promised she'd get to watch him suffer through all the holiday fun. Looks like she'd get her chance. He came back from the kitchen and grabbed her plate and his sister's, since she was done. He stopped when Gabby added, "We could go ice skating as well. There's an outdoor rink downtown." She folded her hands together, her gaze beaming at Owen.

He set the plate down and walked over to Gabby, coming up behind her chair and leaning low, over her shoulder. "That's a great idea, babe," he said for everyone to hear. Under the guise of kissing her cheek, he leaned in, his lips hovering so close to her ear he brushed it and felt her shiver. "Payback, Gabby?"

She chuckled and turned her face so they were eye to eye. Despite her laugher, there was something else in her gaze. "Absolutely, *babe,*" she whispered back.

"I don't know if I'm up to ice skating, but I can take pictures," Patty said.

Owen backed up, his thoughts a bit fuzzy, like they were running into each other head on. She'd called him 'babe'. No one had ever called him that. He liked it. Owen resumed clearing the table and worried one of two things was happening: he and Gabby were extremely good at pretending, or he was experiencing some surprisingly strong chemistry with his best friend.

Both options scared him.

They finished up their card game when the kitchen was back to normal. He took some teasing from his family about how he still needed everything in order. What was wrong with being organized and neat? More than once, Gabby defended his penchant for clean, making his heart squeeze. She always had his back.

"I need some sleep," Patty announced. Owen's stomach cramped. They hadn't sorted out sleeping arrangements. How had he forgotten? *Because they weren't supposed to be here until tomorrow and I was going to talk to Gabby tonight.*

He and Gabby looked at each other. She spoke first. "I should get going, too. Let you all get settled and visit. I have a pull-out couch, so a couple of you can bunk there. I'll go make it up."

"What do you mean get going?" Beth asked, looking up from the corner of the couch where she was knitting with a dark green wool.

Gabby widened her eyes, silently asking Owen to step in. He tried to, but he didn't know what solution to offer, so no words left his mouth. He had a second bedroom, but other than some workout equipment he rarely used, it was bare. He preferred having his office in front of the windows, close to the kitchen. And he'd thought of picking up an air mattress but had gotten sidetracked. Gabby was glaring at him. He grimaced and hoped his shrug came across as apologetic.

His dad gave a deep laugh. "I think we're old enough to know you two aren't spending nights in your own beds. No need to change the routine for us. Why don't your mother and I sleep across the hall in Gabby's bedroom, if that's okay with her, and Patty and Ophelia can take her couch? Then you two have the apartment to yourselves again."

Owen bit back his sigh of relief. This could work. He and Gabby would be alone, and he'd just offer to take the couch and give her his bed. He'd get up before his family came back over in the morning. Before he could speak, Ophelia caught his eye, giving him a similar look to the one Gabby just had. Gabby clearly picked up on the fact that Lia didn't want to bunk with her aunt.

Her cheeks were that sweet shade of red he liked seeing, but her voice was strong when she said, "We really don't need the apartment to ourselves. Ophelia, why don't you sleep here on Owen's couch, and your parents and aunt can have my place? I'll just go over and change my sheets, and get some blankets out for Patty to bunk in my living room." She rose from the couch.

"You shouldn't go to all that trouble for us. Let me make up the beds," Beth said.

"I'll help, too," Patty said.

Gabby shook her head and Owen saw the tension in her face. "No. Please. I need to grab a few things anyway. Besides, you're guests. I would never ask you to do that."

"Aw, come on. We've had a meal, we're sharing Christmas together, and you love our son. I think we're more than guests," his dad said. Owen's stomach lurched as his dad added, "We're family."

She *was* family. In an entirely different way than any of the others, but no less important. In fact, in many ways, she was more. Because he couldn't imagine going a week without seeing her, never mind the months he went without his family. Owen felt like he was being squeezed in a vice from the inside out.

His mind was in overdrive as everyone started to move and grab suitcases. He caught Gabby's arm as she was heading out the door.

His palms felt sweaty so he let her go before he whispered, "Gabs? What are we doing? Where will you sleep?"

She stopped and looked up at him. Putting one hand on his chest, she whispered back, "Exactly where your family expects me to. With my boyfriend." He couldn't read the smile on her face, but his traitorous body was a big fan of her answer.

Chapter Eight

Gabby didn't want to think about what was to come. *As if you haven't thought about it a million times already.* She'd imagined it and fantasized about spending the night in his bed, but never like this. Not once had she pictured lying beside Owen all night pretending she was his girlfriend while his sister slept steps away on the couch. But it was so clear Ophelia didn't want to sleep beside Patty. What could she do? If they really were a couple, it would have seemed silly to need the apartment to themselves and make the two women share a bed. She yanked the corner of the fitted sheet around the end of the bed. She had a new understanding of the phrase "take one for the team." *Stupid. Stupid. Why did you think you could do this? All night lying beside him?* Grabbing the top sheet, she waved it up and down in the air, trying to straighten it across the bed. *What if he sleeps naked? Even if he does, he won't while you're here.* Which was a shame. *No, not a shame. Sanity saving. It'll be hard enough lying next to him dressed for bed.*

Her bedroom door opened and shut quickly. Owen stood against the door, hair slightly disheveled, a wary look in his eyes. Oh, God. She didn't need him in her bedroom. She needed five minutes away from him before she spent the night with him. Was that too much to ask? She wished she had the equivalent of a hazmat suit. *Someone should invent that. Put this on and the lust you feel for your best friend will go unnoticed. Likewise, the sexy scent of his soap will not seep into your skin.*

Her tone was clipped, but she couldn't help it. "What are you doing in here?" She yanked the blanket up the bed and Owen grabbed the pillows from where she'd tossed them on the floor.

"Apologizing. Gabby, I didn't think this all the way through. I'm sorry. I've put you in a stupidly awkward position. I can't even believe I didn't think about this. On the upside, my family loves you."

The muscles around her heart tightened. It was hard enough to pretend she didn't love-love Owen, but *not* falling for his family was an impossible feat. He was so different from them, yet he fit. He didn't think he did, but as an outsider, she could see the truth. Gabby hated feeling like she didn't *fit*. Anywhere. At least, not for real. Being with them could make her forget that. For this week, anyway.

"They're great. I'm not sure how you ended up being wound so tight, but they love you and it shows. I feel like you should have time alone with them, though, so maybe I'll make myself somewhat scarce," Gabby said. She took the coward's way out and used the act of plumping the pillows to avoid Owen's gaze.

He stepped closer, bent his knees to try and catch her gaze. "Uh-uh. No way. You're their favorite thing about me right now. And I'll let the wound-so-tight comment go, for now. Come on. We should get back. Patty needs some sleep. You're not mad, are you?"

He came all the way around the bed and turned her so

they were facing each other. She pasted on a smile. "Nope. Why would I be mad? So we sleep side by side for the night. It's not like you've never seen me in my pajamas."

Owen laughed. "That's true. You do favor them over a lot of your other clothing. But really, this matters a lot to me, so thank you."

Gabby pulled her lip between her teeth, using the pressure to stop herself from blurting out something she couldn't take back. It was one week. She spent dozens of nights next to him on the couch or across the table eating dinner. They were friends. *Friends. Catch a ball game friends. Order pizza, binge watch Netflix friends, "hey, can you grab me this when you run to the store?" friends.* She was completely comfortable with him. Even after she'd realized her feelings were beyond the friendship zone, she had no trouble maintaining her emotions.

It had happened without permission, almost gradually, so she'd had no control, no ability to stop it. But the moment it had hit her was like a burst of light and color—fireworks. He had been leaning over her at her computer, explaining how to find some documents she'd lost. He'd started reprimanding her about internet safety and computer viruses. She'd looked up, saw he was perfectly serious, and she found it so absolutely adorable, it stole her breath. And she knew. She knew this man standing over her, one hand on the back of her chair, one hand pointing at her security settings, that he was exactly what she wanted.

Without meaning to, she'd come to rely on his company, his opinion, his quiet acceptance of who she was. He knew how to make her laugh and when she needed to be alone. It had been so long since someone *knew* her, and there was such comfort in that familiarity. She wouldn't jeopardize what they had. She couldn't. Without him...she couldn't think about that. When she'd lost her parents and had surfaced from the grief enough to function, she'd carried blame and self-hatred with her like a security blanket. She told herself she didn't deserve a family.

When she and Owen grew closer, he'd become the only family she'd ever had as an adult. And now, there was his actual family, who were funny and interesting and downright charming. It was impossible not to feel a connection with them. Doing things Owen's way let her have a piece of something she'd craved. *Which will make it harder when this is done.* If they hadn't lied, Gabby could have become part of his family as a friend. It was too late now. Playing make-believe would have to suffice, because actually being more than friends with Owen and having it not work out would break her. Patty had been right; she'd had enough loss, and Gabby didn't know if she could recover from losing Owen, too. So it was a risk she wouldn't take. She tried to imagine telling him the truth and shook her head. He'd practically jumped away from her when she'd taken the kiss too far last night.

Telling him she loved him for real would be like locking a vault she didn't have the code to. She'd never get back in.

So she'd do exactly what she said she would and hope the couple of drama classes she'd taken in college would help her pull off her dream role. Owen held out a hand and she took it. When he squeezed, the sensation vibrated right up her arm to her heart. They walked back to find his family laughing loudly over a story Ophelia was sharing.

They said goodnights and shared more hugs—they were like competitive huggers or something—and finally, they were in Owen's room. She could hear him brushing his teeth and knew she had a problem when even that sounded endearing. Gabby crawled between his sheets, inhaling the scent of him that lingered on his pillow. When she caught herself trying to trap the scent in her chest, she groaned. Sitting up, she grabbed the offending pillow and squished it together before slamming it back down on the bed, punching it a few times with the side of her fist.

"What did my pillow ever do to you?" Owen was leaning in the archway of the bathroom door, smirking at her. He wore plaid pajama bottoms and a loose fit T-shirt. His hair was mussed from pulling the shirt over his head. When he climbed in beside her, Gabby curled her fingers into his bedspread, denying the urge to reach up and run her hand through the thick strands. Her heart played like a drum solo.

Tonight would be like the mornings she let herself stop at the café on the way to work. She always, always wanted an extra doughnut, but she talked herself out of it, every time. Because she didn't need two. One was enough. And sleeping next to Owen, pretending he loved her, just so he could make his family happy, was enough. Because more would be too much. And like the extra doughnut, she'd regret it. She didn't need Owen any more than she needed delicious, high-calorie foods. Plenty of people got by in life without doughnuts. Or Owens.

She shifted, unable to find a piece of the bed that didn't smell like him. Being with Owen, for real, would only end badly, Gabby reminded herself. She couldn't handle another relationship where she wasn't enough. She'd been through that with Roger and she knew Owen wanted so much more than what Gabby had to offer. And less in some areas. She didn't need added heartache any more than she needed the extra sugary treats. Though now, she really wanted both. She sighed into the pillow.

"You okay?" His voice whispered in the dark. He'd shut out the light and rolled to face her.

Inching her bottom back to the edge of the bed, she tried to hold her breath, but couldn't do that *and* talk. They weren't touching, but she could feel him, and if she closed her eyes, the scent of his soap and toothpaste and his skin surrounded her. "Yes. Are you?"

"Mostly."

She smiled, not that he could see. "Mostly?"

"Yeah. It's a little odd having you in my bed," he answered.

Her pulse sped up. Gabby found herself wondering who else had shared this bed with him. He was discreet, and though he'd mentioned a few dates here and there since Vanessa, she didn't think he'd…connected with anyone. If she were smart, she'd have pretended to sleep. Instead, she spoke. "It's a little odd to be here. In the place where all the non-prudish action happens." *Oh my God. What is wrong with you?*

Owen laughed, hard. "Yeah. That side of the bed has been quiet for a good long time."

Why did this relieve her so much? She shifted again, settling her hand on the bed between them. His hand covered hers and Gabby went perfectly still. Even her heart paused before picking up speed. She was afraid to move or breathe for fear of interrupting the moment. It was one she wanted to tuck away for lonely nights that would inevitably come. She'd remember the feel of her hand surrounded by his, the weight of it, the way his thumb moved back and forth. With her eyes closed, she listened to the sounds of their combined breathing. Why was this so easy for him?

"Thank you for doing this, Gabs. You're really the best friend anyone could have."

Like a deflated balloon, she whooshed out a breath. "Yeah. Back at you."

Just as she began to nod off, she heard Owen whisper, "You know what's really weird? How comfortable it is to lie beside you like this."

Comfort. Cuddly. Sweet.

She was his teddy bear.

Biting down on her lip, she feigned sleep, letting her breathing settle and even out so she could listen to his. She fell asleep dreaming that her pretend life was real.

Chapter Nine

Gabby could hear Owen and his family even with the door to his bedroom closed. He was being a considerate pretend-boyfriend and letting her sleep. As if she could. She'd tossed and turned for most of the night while he slept soundly. She knew because she watched. Not in a creepy stalker way. Just in an everyday I-love-you-and-want-to-wake-you-up-and-seduce-you sort of way.

She'd feigned sleep when he'd awoken. She'd heard his breathing shift and then felt the bed move as he rolled toward her. Her heart rate had tripled when he'd put his hand on her hip and just lay beside her for a few minutes, and then he was up, quietly moving around his room. She heard him shower and had several indecent thoughts about joining him. Then she'd heard him slip out of the room. He and Ophelia had been quiet, but Gabby didn't think Leo had it in him to keep his voice down. She'd heard him boom a hearty good morning and Gabby smiled into the pillow.

She smelled waffles and bacon. Her stomach growled and she knew she needed to get up, but it was really hard to leave the bed in which she'd spent the night with Owen. If she stayed right where she was, she could imagine it was everything they were pretending to be.

Her eyes were on the door, so when it opened, Owen's gaze latched directly onto hers. His smile was like a kick in the gut. Why was he so freaking sweet and who looked that good in the morning? She didn't want to think about what she looked like with her hair all over his pillow, her face scrubbed of even a hint of makeup, and her eyes likely puffy.

He walked to the side of the bed and sat so her body was curled around his hip. Without a word he put his hand to her hair and smoothed it back from her face. She couldn't read his expression.

"Hey," she whispered.

Owen let his hand wander to her arm and rest there, on her biceps, like it was the most natural thing in the world. He thought he didn't fit in with his theatrical family, but in Gabby's eyes, he deserved an award for acting.

"Good morning, sleepyhead."

Gabby curled her fingers together under the pillow so she didn't reach out and touch his thigh. Or any other part of him. "Sorry. You're all up and I'm being lazy. Your bed is way more comfortable than mine," she said. It wasn't a lie.

"Don't be sorry. It's the holidays. We made breakfast, though, and it's ready."

"I could smell it in my sleep," she said, trying for a smile.

He tapped the tip of her nose with his index finger. "No surprise there. If you were a princess in a fairy tale, it wouldn't be true love's kiss that would wake you, it'd be the scent of your favorite foods."

Gabby laughed even though her heart pinched painfully. "A combination of the two would make the best fairy tale."

She'd meant it as a joke, but Owen looked at her like she'd grown an extra head or something. And then slowly, like she *was* still dreaming, he leaned forward and touched his lips to hers, so soft and quick it was like it never happened. When he pulled back, he gave her a crooked grin.

"Time to get up, Princess Gabby."

She couldn't speak. He didn't seem to notice. He rose from the bed and pulled his phone from the back pocket of his jeans. Frowning down at it, he muttered, "Huh."

Gabby sat up. "What is it?"

Owen glanced up as he texted. "Brady says they're having a quick meeting down in the lobby in about thirty minutes."

"A meeting for what?"

"Don't know. Better get up, though. We'll eat and go down. I'll tell him you're with me, okay?"

She nodded and he left, texting as he went. *So much for being a princess.* Throwing back the covers, she got out of bed, righted the blankets, and changed into something presentable. She'd have to shower later since clearly, she had several other things on today's agenda.

Gabby ended up sneaking in an express shower after breakfast. She told Owen she'd meet him downstairs. When she left his apartment, his family was sitting around his table, planning out their "Family Day of Festive Fun." Beth had actually put that as a title.

The lobby was crowded and noisy. It wasn't a huge building, but when all the tenants gathered together, it seemed like it. People were talking and a few called out a hello. Gabby waved, then saw Owen near Mr. Bramby, the man who'd lived here longer than any of them. The older man was wearing his go-to charcoal gray jogging suit, which was quirky enough. Add in the fedora he never left home without and he was very interesting to look at. One day, Gabby wanted to paint him, or at least his hat.

Owen waved and made his way through the crowd. Gabby was hearing snippets of conversation, but couldn't really follow any of them.

"Hey, babe, there you are," Owen said. She froze for a second, wondering if he was staying in character or had just forgotten himself. Before she could think too much about it, he leaned in and kissed her cheek, very near her lips. If she'd turned her head just a little, their mouths would have met. Had he called her endearing terms before they'd become faux boyfriend and girlfriend? It felt so right she thought maybe he did, but why hadn't she noticed? *You'd have noticed.* The sound of sweetie or babe coming from his lips made her stomach do a delicious dip. *Don't get used to it.*

Gabby rolled her shoulders as she surveyed the crowd. "So? What's going on?"

She spotted Mr. Grumpy—aka Wyatt—leaning one shoulder against the far wall. His arms were crossed over his chest and his ever-present frown was plastered on his face. Owen once said he thought he was a mob hitman. Brady dared him to ask. But now that she'd spoken to him, despite his intimidating glower and impressive height, he didn't seem like a mob boss or hitman to Gabby. Not that she had any experience with that kind of thing, but she had gut instinct. Wyatt's eyes surveyed the crowd and landed on Gabby. He arched an eyebrow and she smiled and waved. She nearly laughed when he shook his head. If she wasn't mistaken, he may even have rolled his eyes.

"Maybe I'll tell you what's going on when you finish flirting with the mobster," Owen hissed. His breath warmed her ear and she leaned in a little closer.

Tilting her head, she asked, "What are you talking about?"

Owen looked across the room then back at Gabby. His eyes were heated—dark. Intense, like he actually felt...

jealous? That couldn't be right. But his hand came around Gabby's waist in a possessive hold. More pretending? Why did pretend feel so good? She was aware of each individual fingertip sinking into her skin.

Owen squeezed gently. "I'm talking about you and Mr. Mean over there making eyes at each other."

Gabby laughed and looked up to meet Owen's eyes. Was he serious? Frustration prickled over her skin. His family wasn't around to fall for their act, so why did he have to push it every minute?

"Oh, please. Would you stop? I really don't think he's *connected*. And, his name is Wyatt." Because she felt inexplicably irritated, she waved again, but Wyatt's expression didn't change.

Owen grabbed her arm and pulled it to her side. "We don't know anything about him."

"You do a really good impression of a jealous boyfriend, O. Please don't pretend to break up with me. I promise I'll stop not-flirting with the non-mobster if you'll just—"

Her words were cut off by Owen's lips smashing against hers with a quiet demand that had her pressing into him. Maybe melting was a better word, because she felt like she was absorbing right into his own body. His hand on her waist clenched, tightening as his mouth slanted across hers. He stole her breath, literally. But she was happy to give it up if it meant getting to kiss him. *Good lord. Where does a self-professed shy geek learn to kiss like this?* Just when she'd have liked to wrap both arms around him, and maybe even her legs, he pulled back.

Breathing heavily, he kept his forehead on hers. "Not everything is pretend, Gabby. Some things are serious."

She didn't know what he meant, but didn't get a chance to ask. Brady wandered over and clapped them both on their backs. "There's my favorite *couple*," he said.

Tall, with dark blond hair he kept fairly short, Brady was good looking and charming. He had a great smile and happy eyes. Everyone liked Brady because he liked everyone. His words made her choke. She looked at Owen, then back at Brady. They didn't have that many friends in common, but it never occurred to her to say something to Brady.

Owen gave Brady a small shove. "Don't be an ass. Don't worry, Gabs. I told him what's going on."

Something stronger than irritation bubbled in her chest. Great. Though she'd rather he knew the truth so it was one less person they were lying to. Brady grinned, crossing his muscular arms across his chest. "He sure did. One of my mechanics is having a get-together tonight. I could use a gorgeous woman on my arm. Want to pretend with me, too?"

Owen's eyes darkened, but it smoothed Gabby's temper and she smirked, pretending to consider it.

It was petty, but she liked the thought of Owen being jealous. "Will there be food?"

Brady gave a wide, self-assured grin. "I'm pretty sure. If not, I promise to feed you."

Owen linked their hands. Gabby wondered why Brady's fun flirting didn't make her tummy flutter the way Owen holding her hand did.

He squeezed her fingers. "Very funny, you two. You can knock it off any time now."

Brady clapped Owen on the back. "Come to think of it, I'm considering taking a beach vacation and I could use someone to rub lotion on my back. Any chance you're free?"

While Gabby laughed, Owen scowled and said, "My two closest friends are now a comedy duo. Lucky me. Feel free to shut it down any time." He looked at Gabby and she tried to muffle her laughter. "You, too."

Brady chuckled, clapped Owen on the back, and winked at Gabby. "Possessive, isn't he?"

Before Gabby could think much about that, Jake stood on a chair and cupped his hands over his mouth.

"Okay, listen up, everyone. Guys, shut the hell up," His white T-shirt was dirty and his jeans hung too low on his hips. Wyatt watched him like an animal stalking its prey. *Hmm. Maybe not a mobster, but clearly not a Jake fan.*

Brady's frown now matched Owen's. He glared at Jake from afar. "I hate that guy," Brady said.

"Because he's a lowlife?" Owen asked. Brady nodded and held out his fist, in sync with his friend again. Owen smirked and bumped fists with him.

The crowd quieted and Jake continued. "I talked to the owner. The cops have done whatever it is they do. The owner will file an insurance claim. I need each of you to write down what you know about what happened and if anything of yours is missing. Then I need you to sign those write-ups and get them in to me by tomorrow. The owner, Mr. Kendrick, said officers would be coming to collect the statements." Questions erupted and Jake yelled for people to be quiet but he'd lost his command of the crowd.

Gabby's pulse scrambled. *Wait. What?* She thought this was a tenants meeting, like she'd suggested. Gripping Owen's arm, she tugged him closer. "The cops? What's he talking about? What's going on?"

Owen's eyebrows furrowed like they did sometimes when he couldn't figure something out. "Sorry. I forgot to say when you got down here. Our storage room was trashed. Someone has been inside every box and a lot of stuff got broken or at least damaged. Not only that, a few neighbors say some of their things are missing entirely."

Gabby's mouth dropped open. The residents began murmuring, with some calling out questions. Unease spread like a virus, washing over Gabby.

"We've been robbed? By someone who lives here?" Her

thoughts whipped back to the mailboxes. She'd forgotten all about them.

Owen's arm went around her shoulder and pulled her close. "Looks like it. The police were pulling away when I got here. Not sure who called."

"Mrs. Haverman. She went to get her cat carrier and found boxes opened, stuff everywhere," Brady said.

Owen shook his head, concern etched on his face. "It feels weird to think a neighbor would do this. Just goes to show you, living in the same place doesn't mean you know someone. You think you do because of the proximity but really, everyone here is a stranger with an untold truth."

Gabby looked up at him, knowing he was correct—even more so than he could imagine. But she didn't want to think like that, so she took his hand and squeezed it. No matter what the distance or what she held back, she and Owen weren't strangers. He didn't know everything in her heart, nor did he need to. But at least they knew, with absolute certainty, they could trust each other. The same couldn't be said for most of the other faces around them.

"Owen," she said, tugging on his arm. "The mailboxes."

Some of the neighbors were shouting questions to Jake and his eye rolls and sighs made it clear he didn't want to be bothered with them.

Brady looked at Gabby, his tone worrying her. "What about the mailboxes?"

Surely someone else had seen them. "They've been tampered with." She looked at Owen. "I meant to say something yesterday, but your family showed up and I forgot."

"Shit," Brady said. "I'll go take a look. I saw one of the officers give Jake a card. I'll call and update them on that."

When he walked through the small group of people, toward the mailboxes, Gabby turned back to Owen. "This is crazy. Why would anyone do this?"

He shrugged. "I don't know. Do you have anything down there that needs to be moved? Anything valuable?"

Gabby had learned, in a devastating way, what was valuable in life. She pressed herself against Owen's body, grateful for the easy way he pulled her closer. "No." Everything of value in her life, other than her art, was right here, in her grasp. She held tighter, scared to let him go. When his hands soothed over her back, she focused on the fact that, at least for now, she didn't have to.

Chapter Ten

"Maybe you two ought to consider another building," Beth suggested, as they all climbed into the rental Owen had arranged through Brady. His truck sat five if three people squeezed into the back seat. Brady owned his own auto shop and had connections, which made the outing with everyone a lot easier. *Really didn't think some of these things through.* He'd been so focused on his lie and getting Gabby to agree, he hadn't thought ahead about some of the logistics.

"Are you considering it now?" Beth asked from the backseat as Owen pulled onto the street. Gabby laughed from the passenger seat beside him.

"Mom, it's a great building. Gabby and I both love it there. This is some anomaly that's been blown out of proportion," Owen said.

His mom lowered her voice, which was completely pointless. "You can't keep an eye on her all the time, Owen. I mean, she's still keeping her own apartment."

Now everyone else joined in on the laughter. Owen's thoughts stuttered. "We, uh, like the space. But it's temporary."

Please don't ask which part. He didn't like lying to his family—he didn't want to. Gabby shot him a side-glance, like she was inside his brain. He thought of just telling his family the truth now; this minute. But he didn't know what the truth was. He'd started this, obviously not thinking the finer details through and now, his heart and his mind were like tilt-a-whirls.

Was there any chance he and Gabby could be the real thing? He didn't want to freak her out by asking while his family was there. This morning, when he'd awoken beside her, a sense of rightness had filled his entire body. It wasn't just the sexual awareness—though that was an eye-opener too—he'd never be able to go back to seeing her as just Gabby now that he realized how much sensuality she exuded without even trying. No, it was more. He'd wanted to pull her tight against him this morning and kiss her awake. He'd settled for putting his hand on her hip, a torture in itself. Then he'd left the bed, trying to shake off the thoughts in the shower. Turned out thinking about Gabby in his shower was not the best plan for getting her out of his head.

"Owen," Gabby hissed.

He was completely freaking himself out. "Sorry. Mom. Everything is fine. It's good. Mall first and then skating?"

"Are we eating lunch at the mall?" Ophelia asked. Owen could see her in the rearview mirror, sitting next to Aunt Patty. She smiled at him. Gabby turned and looked at his sister.

"See, that's what we should be thinking about, not the building," Gabby said playfully.

"I love a girl who can eat," Leo said.

Owen couldn't disagree, though he hadn't given it much thought before now. "Mall, it is," he said, flipping the signal and changing lanes.

Owen finished up his chow mein, which was surprisingly good for mall food. He was just starting to relax and feel like maybe his mom's family-festive-whatever day was not such a bad idea. She'd run to the washroom with Aunt Patty. His dad was checking out smart phones at one of the booths. He and Gabby and Ophelia were chatting about theater—specifically, Owen's dislike of being in the limelight.

"He's actually pretty good on stage," Ophelia said, biting on the end of her straw.

Owen scoffed. "One show. Fifth grade. I played a turkey in a Thanksgiving play. I have no idea how you're even counting that and have a sneaking suspicion you only brought it up to embarrass me."

Gabby laughed and popped another fry in her mouth. "A turkey? I can picture that."

He scowled at her, but really, he was loving the fact that his sister and his girl—whoa, what the hell? His *best friend* and his sister were getting along so well. He sat up, wishing he'd worn just a T-shirt instead of a sweater. It was hot as hell in the food court.

"Funny," Owen said.

"Seriously, though, he's read with me more than once when I needed help. He's a good actor."

Owen's breath froze in his lungs. Gabby's lips firmed into a line and she nodded. With her head down, like her French fries were the most interesting things ever, she mumbled her words. "Oddly enough, I can picture that, too."

He reached out and put his hand over hers, his heart splitting at the tone of her voice. He'd never hurt her on purpose. Had something about this hurt her? He couldn't say anything, and his mother picked that moment to come rushing back with his aunt.

"Let's go. Clean up. I have a surprise," Beth said.

Patty chuckled, her cheeks rosy, not so pale today. "Boy,

do you."

Owen glanced up, narrowing his eyes at his mom. "What kind of surprise?"

Ophelia stood, laughing at him as she started gathering their trays. "Probably the surprise kind. Just go with it."

When Owen looked at Gabby, she shrugged and began helping his sister. He couldn't shake the feeling that something was wrong.

Tidying their spot, which was scooped the second they walked away from the table, they followed his mother and aunt, found his dad along the way and headed toward the center of the mall. Their bags and jackets hung from their arms as they weaved in and out of the slew of shoppers. Had no one shopped early?

They stopped at Santa's Village. *No. Please, no.*

His mother turned, like she was ten instead of in her sixties, clapped her hands together, and squealed. *Squealed.* Jesus. Owen ducked his head because people were actually looking at them.

"What do you have there, Beth?" Leo asked. He took the white ticket she was holding. "Well, we haven't done this in a while, kids." His dad was beaming because he apparently had no issue with his wife's goofiness.

Owen knew even before his mom spoke. "We're getting our picture with Santa," his mom said. "I've already paid, so we get to skip the line."

Gabby and Ophelia laughed and really, all he could do was shake his head. Gabby grabbed his hand and squeezed it. "I haven't sat on Santa's lap since I was in elementary school." There was nothing that could have brought out his own genuine enthusiasm more than the smile on her face or the excited tone of her voice. A tender ache settled just below his heart, making his rib cage feel too tight. Too small.

He took her hand, twined their fingers, letting himself

absorb the knowledge, the truth, that his feelings for Gabriella, whatever they had been, had definitely crossed a line. Going with instinct, as he had that morning, or more, with need, he cupped her cheek in his palm and pressed a kiss to her lips. "Then let's go," he said.

There were a few people ahead of them in the pre-paid line. Ophelia bumped shoulders with him while Gabby talked to his dad about attending a theater performance.

"I like her," Ophelia said quietly.

Owen turned his head so he was looking at his sister. "Me too. Lots to like." More than he ever could have imagined.

"Must have been a quick transition," Ophelia said. He could tell when she was digging.

He shrugged.

It didn't put her off. "You just woke up one morning and thought, nope, friendship isn't enough?"

His pulse scrambled. *Yeah. Basically, this morning.* "Something like that." He put a hand to her back and nudged her forward. "Our turn, let's go see Santa."

Ophelia laughed loudly. "Words I have not heard from you in a long time."

Santa's eyes widened a bit when he saw the six of them heading toward him. *Don't worry, big guy, no way are all of us sitting on your lap.* Owen was willing to go along, but he had boundaries.

Apparently, so did his dad. Leo took a step up onto Santa's platform, and squeezed himself to the right of the oversized red chair, in between a giant snowflake and a fake tree. "I'll stand back here. Son, get on the other side."

"Ho, ho, ho. Not often I get all grown-ups," Santa said, adding a few more ho-ho-hos. "Have you been good?"

"Owen hasn't," Ophelia said, standing in front of him, also to Santa's side.

"She lies," Owen said. His gut cramped. *Actually, I do. To the people I love.*

Gabby went to the other side and Patty and his mom each took a knee. Owen's lunch threatened to return when Patty smiled widely at Santa and gave his beard a playful tug.

"Careful, Santa," she said, "I'm newly single so I might get the wrong idea."

Fortunately, Santa gave a few more deep chuckles and the woman taking the picture grabbed their attention.

They smiled and it was over. Easy as that. *See. I can be fun and spontaneous.* He was about to say so to Gabby and his sister when his mother took Gabby's hand.

"We'll move out of the way. I want one of just you two with Santa," she said. She and Patty stepped down. Ophelia did as well. Leo pulled himself out of the winter wonderland and stood beside his mom.

Owen closed his eyes and counted to three. If he wished really hard, maybe he'd disappear. Even if Gabby was only pretending to be his girlfriend, he didn't need his mom providing fodder for years of teasing to come.

Gabby was biting her lip when he opened his eyes. His sister nudged him in the shoulder.

"You can show it to your kids one day," she said, laughing at him.

His mother made a swooning noise. "Yes, please. Lots of grandbabies. I worried you'd never find a girl and give them to me."

But his gaze was on Gabby so he noticed the way her eyes dimmed, the way her smile faltered and she lowered her chin. He took her hand and pulled her closer.

"You okay with this?"

"Sure. Why not?" She pulled her hand from his and took a seat on Santa's left knee.

"You go over there, honey," his mom said.

As if there's another choice, Mom. He wanted to look at

Gabby, but the photographer was waiting for them. He had a feeling his smile was tight.

"You two make sure you're good," Santa said.

"You, too, Santa," Gabby said. Her tone was no longer playful, but since his mother was nowhere near done with her plans, Owen wouldn't have a chance to talk to her anytime soon.

Chapter Eleven

After shopping, they went for hot chocolate and listened to carolers in the park. There was an indoor/outdoor nursery next to the park and they'd supplied decorations for a Christmas tree decorating contest. It had been pretty amusing to watch, and a few of the trees had turned out beautifully. They'd spent so long there, they'd decided to forgo the skating, which Owen was secretly happy about. Did he really need Gabby seeing him fall flat on his ass?

By the time they returned to his apartment, it was time for dinner. Gabby helped his mom and Patty in the kitchen while his dad watched television. After dinner, Gabby snuck away with her sketch pad. Owen was in the middle of a card game with his sister while his dad snored on the couch. His mom and Patty had gone over to Gabby's to watch a movie. Bing played softly around his dad's noisy sleeping. It was like a time warp had sent him back to 1995. His mind kept wandering to Gabby, but he knew to leave her when the mood struck. Sometimes she'd be gone for hours, madly creating whatever vision only she could see. He'd seen her pour her heart onto the canvas and been there in the moments afterward where she seemed physically drained from the effort.

"Gabby okay?" Ophelia said. She tossed the card she'd picked up onto the discard pile and flipped one of the ones in front of her.

Owen smiled. "Yeah. She's like you when you bury yourself into a character. Sometimes she can't pull herself out." Owen flipped his card, then eyed his sister's. She was going to beat him again.

"So, earlier, I asked you about getting together with her. In all the texts we've sent, you never mentioned when things shifted between you two," Ophelia said.

Owen took his turn. "Is that a question?"

Ophelia laughed. "Is there an answer? You never said how you two decided to cross over from friendship." She laid down her final card, showing a score of zero.

Owen shook his head and wrote down their respective scores. "It just sort of happened, you know?"

"We'd know more if you actually gave some details. Did you ask her out? Take her on a date?" Ophelia pulled all of the cards in and shuffled them.

"Obviously we've been out. It just…transitioned. That's all. The way some things do."

An itch started under his skin. The conversation was unnerving. He didn't want to tell more lies. Especially since the original lie was starting to feel more like the truth.

"I think I'll call it a night," he said, just as she started to deal.

Ophelia snorted, a clear sign she knew a retreat when she saw one.

Owen thought he'd find Gabby curled up on the oversized

chair in his bedroom, sketchbook in hand. He had looked forward to seeing her there like that, he realized. Instead, she was sitting in the middle of his bed, in a pair of pajama shorts and a tank top, laughing at whatever album she seemed to be flipping through.

"Hey," he said, ignoring the warmth crowding his chest. He shut the door behind him and arched an eyebrow when she slapped the album shut and put it behind her back. *No. Mom wouldn't have...*

"Hi." She scooted back on the bed, pushing the dark blue album, which he now recognized, under the pillow.

"Gabby. What are you doing? You were supposed to be sketching," he said, advancing.

If it was possible to look down her nose at him while she looked up at him, she managed. "Is that what I was *supposed* to be doing? I didn't know I had to confirm my activities with you."

His legs hit the bed and Gabby's body tensed, like she was ready to spring from the mattress. With the album, most likely.

His heart dove into his stomach. "Did my mother give you that?"

Her smile started slow then took over her entire face. Her eyes shone with it. She nodded.

Oh, Mom so did. He thrust out his hand. "Give it."

"Oh, no. It's too good. There are actual bath shots, O. And the time you dressed up as your sister. And there's one shot of you learning how to pee standing up," she said. Her words came out slightly muffled as her hand shot to her mouth to cover the fit of laughter.

He launched himself at the album, but she tugged it away just in time and he landed on top of her. The album went flying to the floor and Gabby laughed, twisting in his arms, trying to get away.

"You think that's funny?"

She nodded. "I really do. I think I'd like to do a new series. Owen: the younger years. From print to paint." Gabby's body convulsed in laughter. She struggled with him as he tickled her and tried to get her to promise never to do such a thing. It didn't take long for her to cave.

"Okay. I promise. Stop. I promise."

"Say 'I swear on my favorite set of brushes to erase all memories of what I saw in Owen's baby book,'" he said, pinning her hands above her head.

She bit her lip, considering. "Owen, I will never, in my life, forget what I saw in those pictures. In fact, in times of trouble or sadness, I may purposely recall them," she said. He tickled again, his fingers grazing her breast accidentally on the way up her arm. She squealed. "Okay. Okay." He paused. "I swear on my favorite set of brushes to never use the images I will forever hold dear as the subject of any of my artwork. Ever."

Owen stopped fighting his grin. He groaned as he collapsed to the side of her, letting her hands go. "Good enough. I can't believe she gave you that."

Though he'd let her wrists go, their bodies were still plastered together as they both tempered their breathing. He felt every curve, every dip, the softness of her body against his own. She whispered, "Best Christmas present ever."

Trying, with everything in him, to keep it light, he pinched her side. "Not funny, Gabs."

"Ow." She rolled to face him so the front of her was pressed to the front of him. As her warm breath fanned over his face, the desire to kiss her, the *need* to kiss her, was a living, breathing thing. Instead of moving back as he should, giving her the space she deserved, his hand rested on her hip. His thumb stroked the tiny strip of skin exposed between her shorts and shirt. He told himself that the shiver he felt rush through her wasn't from his touch. Because, while he was busy falling, she was just doing him a favor.

He looked at her lips, which were slightly parted. There was no way she couldn't feel the effect lying so close was having on him. For some perverse reason, he squeezed her hip, which moved her even closer. Gabby's eyes widened. There was a reason they'd never crossed this line. He hated chaos, he hated change. Doing anything right this minute, giving in to the lust swirling inside him like a tempest would not only change everything, it would throw his life into chaos. He and Gabby were perfect. *As friends*.

He didn't believe in staying friends with exes. Relationships ended for a reason and were best left in the past. But if things took a wrong turn with Gabby, she'd leave a hole unlike any other woman. He'd dated enough women to know what they had was beyond special. It was everything.

Could he risk that to see where this led for real? Would she even want to try? He was about to give in to the aching need to roll her onto her back and kiss the air out of her, to explore every inch of her body until neither of them could move or speak or think, despite his own warnings, when she spoke.

"You've really closed your family out, Owen. I don't understand why." Her hand rested on his chest.

"What do you mean?"

"It's like you don't want them to know you," she said. Her gaze moved from his chest, over his face, then finally settled on his eyes. "You're different than them, but they love you. They *see* you and accept you. Or they would if you let them in. They want to be part of your life and lying to them, letting them believe things that will never happen, isn't fair."

He moved his hand up and down her side, not sure if he was soothing her or himself. "It's only for a week, Gabs. It's not a big deal. It's not like I'm hiding some deep, shameful secret for fear of their response. I just didn't want to deal with having lied to my mom about a girlfriend. Especially not over the holidays and with Patty's situation. I didn't think it was that big of a deal." It wouldn't have been if all these feelings hadn't rained down on him like a freaking storm.

Her lips pressed tightly together and he wished the urge to kiss them would lessen.

"That's not what I'm talking about," she said.

He waited, but she said nothing. "Then what?"

With a growl of frustration, she pulled away from him and sat up. Pulling her knees to her chest, her hair formed a curtain around them. He didn't trust himself to avert his gaze from her face. There was no way her shorts wouldn't be riding up. He had to work at staying with the conversation.

"Kids."

That pulled him all the way in. "Excuse me?"

"Your parents think you want kids. They said we'd show our Santa picture to them someday. Did you never tell them you don't?"

It was his turn to sit up. "What are you talking about?"

She pushed a hand through her hair but it fell back immediately. "You broke up with your last girlfriend because she wanted children and it didn't fit into your perfectly plotted life. You've let them believe not only in us, which is bad enough and I feel guilty about it, but in the idea that you'll one day give them grandchildren. It's selfish. Stop hiding from them. Just tell them the truth. It's cowardly not to."

Emotions battled in his chest. Anger led the way. "I'll repeat, what the hell are you talking about, Gabriella?" Why the hell would she think he didn't want kids? And if he didn't, which he damn well did, she thought he'd hide that from the people he loved? Was that how Gabby saw him? Did she really think he was so much of a coward he wouldn't set them straight on something that important? In the back of his mind, he couldn't help thinking what he was making her go through this week was further proof of him being all those things.

Her head snapped up at his tone, but fire burned in her eyes. "You're a lot of things, Owen. But you're not slow. Your family is wonderful and I cannot, for the life of me, figure out why you keep hiding things from them instead of letting them see who you really are."

His mouth dropped open, but Gabby wasn't finished.

"Do they or do they not know that you and Vanessa broke up because of kids?"

She really does think that. As if he'd break up with a woman based on that alone. Owen jumped off the bed and stalked to his closet. He needed a second to breathe, to absorb the fact that the person who supposedly knew him better than anyone apparently thought he was a shallow bastard who would dump a woman for wanting to start a family with him. No, he'd never explicitly divulged the truth to Gabby—because he thought she'd *know*. Because she knew him. She knew he loved kids…didn't she? They were so close, but were there parts of themselves they *didn't* share simply as an awareness of the invisible boundary between friend and lover?

He yanked his shirt over his head, tossing it toward the hamper, not picking it up when he missed. He shucked his jeans next and whipped them in the same direction. Pulling open one of the drawers of the built-in wardrobe, he pulled on a pair of pajama bottoms but was too angry to worry about a shirt.

She was sitting on her knees, her eyes uncertain now. "Owen."

He put his hands on his hips and glared at her. "They know, as I thought you did, that *one* of the reasons I broke it off with Vanessa was because she *didn't* want a family. In case you're unsure, some of the other reasons included her wanting access to my bank account, her annoying laugh, her constant complaining about my job, and the fact that she irritated the hell out of me at the end."

Gabby winced. He didn't lose his temper often, but he couldn't stop himself now. He wanted to shake her and ask her how she could not know something so basic, so fundamental about him. He was overreacting, surely. Shoving his hands into his hair, he paced the length of the room, back and forth in front of the bed.

Her body sagged. "I'm sorry," she whispered.

"For what?"

"For not knowing better. For assuming it was you."

The anger began to wane. He wasn't even sure who he was angrier with. Why should she know what he'd never said? God. Even now he was hiding things from her. How could he tell her, though, that his feelings had shifted?

"Why did you?" he asked.

Her lip quivered and his heart pinched. "She was perfect. I was joking the other day when I was talking about your list, but I know you have one—at least a mental one. And she had it all. Tall, blond, looks like a model, steady, respectable job, looks great in an evening gown or designer jeans, kept up with the news and could have a political discussion." Gabby rolled her eyes at the last point.

When he tried to discuss politics, she did the same thing as when he talked computer codes: she feigned immediate sleep. It always made him laugh. She called it "politics-induced narcolepsy."

A smile worked its way to his lips, but his heart still pounded too hard. She may not have known he wanted children one day, but she'd been bang-on about the rest of his list and it was a hell of a thing to realize she hadn't been entirely wrong—he might actually be a shallow bastard. He realized not one of the things she listed now mattered to him. It wasn't about the list, it was about the person. And the person sitting on his bed was fast becoming the only woman he could imagine wanting.

Gabby sniffled and he saw the first tear fall. Everything else fell away and he was beside her, pulling her into his arms, ignoring the pleasure that spread through him at the feel of her cheek against his bare chest. Her tears burned his skin, knowing he'd been the cause of them.

"Don't cry, babe." His own throat went tight. He couldn't stand to see her cry.

"I'm sorry. Here I am lecturing you and it's like I don't even know you. And even if I do, who am I to tell you how to live your life? I'm sorry. It's none of my business what you choose to tell your family. How you choose to let them view you is up to you. I just hate thinking they're missing out on any part of you because…"

He tilted her chin up, rubbing his thumb along her skin to catch the tear hovering on her cheek. Tenderness swamped him. "Because?"

"Because you're *you*. It's like you only let them in so far so they can't disappoint you or vice versa, but it doesn't work like that when people love you. When you're a family. You're perfect. To the people who love you, you're perfect. They'll accept every part of you because that's what family does. They want what's best for you, even if you can't see it."

His heart seized, making breathing nearly impossible. "Gabby," he said, whispering her name like it was as fragile as she felt in his arms. Here he was merely tolerating his family and she'd spent the last twelve years blaming herself for not having one.

Owen wished he could pull her pain inside himself so she didn't have to carry it all the time. "It wasn't your fault they died."

She tried to pull away as new tears fell, but he locked his arms. "Logically, I know that. But sometimes it hurts so bad I can't breathe. I'd give anything to have them back. To have them butting into my business and forcing us to have pictures with Santa." She half laughed, half sobbed. Without letting her go, Owen snagged the Kleenex box on his nightstand. She wiped her eyes, still sniffling, then took a couple of deep breaths. He brought both of his hands to her face, cradling her cheeks in his palms. Her eyes were bright, making the blue shimmer like water.

"Your parents wouldn't want you to carry around this guilt. You have to let it go. You were a kid; what you did was completely normal. Teenagers sneak out. They go to parties they aren't supposed to, date people they aren't supposed to. It's not your fault a typical teenage rebellion ended so badly. All teens push back. It's how they find themselves."

She sniffled again and he wondered what the hell was wrong with him when she was sitting here crying and he was thinking about how cute she looked with her red nose and crazy hair. She looked...real.

"You never did. I bet you never fought back or went against your parents' wishes. You were probably annoyingly perfect even as a teen."

For the first time since he'd entered his bedroom, the tension inside him eased. He lifted her off the bed, setting her on her feet, and pulled down the covers. He gestured for her to climb in. When she did, he hit the lights and crawled in beside her, very aware of how natural, how right, it felt to be ending the night with her in his bed.

"Ophelia can tell you differently. I'm not perfect, Gabby. You of all people should know that. And honestly, thinking about it, I'm a bit of a jerk."

"You are not!"

He loved the way she defended him no matter what. He chuckled, moving closer to her, catching the hint of vanilla soap she showered with. Owen managed to shut down the image of Gabby in the shower, but he knew he might never get the scent of vanilla out of his bed.

"You were right, what you said about Vanessa and the other girls I've dated. I had some sort of checklist of the kind of woman I figured would lead me to a quiet and happy life." But it would be colorless, he realized.

"A life that includes having children."

"Of course. I love kids."

"But you hate mess and disorder and family functions."

He sighed, rolling onto his back to think about that. He stared at the ceiling even though he couldn't see it and smiled when he felt Gabby's fingers entwine with his own. Her hand was small, elegant. A perfect fit.

"My family is nutty. They require a lot of energy. They *have* a lot of energy. I wasn't always so…particular, but I guess with my job being what it is—working from home—I've become less social. Even more than I meant to, maybe. I've never been the outgoing one in my family. They all want the spotlight and I've always been the one who wanted to stay backstage, out of the glow."

"There's nothing wrong with that, O."

He squeezed her hand. "No. There isn't. But I had a good childhood. I was happy. They embarrassed the hell out of me more times than I can count, but I grew up knowing I was loved. I know I'm lucky and I've always wanted a family. With the right person. I guess I'll have to come around a little on the Martha Stewart tendencies and family get-togethers."

Gabby laughed and leaned her body against his, her head resting on his shoulder. He moved, adjusting his arm so he could slide it under her head. Her cheek pressed against his chest. Her hand rested softly, tentatively, over his heart. Her fingers played with the hair there absently, but he felt the effects rock through his body. It took effort to concentrate on her words.

"That's just it, you shouldn't have to change to

accommodate the people you share your life with. That's what Roger wanted from me. He wanted me to be something I wasn't and when I refused or didn't bother, he walked away. Loving someone doesn't include making them into what you deem lovable. It means wanting them as they are. Wanting the life you would lead with the real them."

Owen's work only enhanced his detail-oriented personality. He didn't make rash decisions. He made pro and con lists. He compared prices and read reviews before making a purchase, even an inconsequential one. He weighed consequences and mapped out possible outcomes. But in that moment, with a barely-there hint of the moon peeking through the blinds and his sister asleep down the hallway, Owen went with his gut. He went with his heart—which he rarely listened to. Perhaps if he had, he would have recognized the feelings sooner.

He rolled to his side, once again adjusting his arm so he could prop himself up on his elbow. His other hand moved to Gabby's waist, stroking the skin that had been taunting him for the past two nights. He could see the shine of her eyes in the dark. He felt her against him, everywhere. Her scent curled inside him. She was part of him and he hadn't taken any time to realize what that actually meant.

"Owen?" Her voice was a whisper.

"There isn't anything about you I would change." He wanted to say more. He wanted to say the words that were tumbling inside his brain and his heart, words he'd held back or buried. But right in that moment, he wanted something more.

Bringing his hand to her face, he smoothed his thumb across her lips. He heard, *felt*, her breath quicken as he inched closer, until looking into her eyes began to consume him and he had to let his own close. His mouth touched hers—not for show or because anyone expected it, but because he needed to kiss her, needed to trace her lips with his tongue and memorize the taste of her. Of Gabby.

Her hand moved up his chest, around the back of his neck and into his hair where her fingers gripped, tightened, like she was afraid he'd get away. There was absolutely nowhere he'd rather be. Using his tongue and his teeth along the column of her neck as he'd wanted to earlier, his fingers drifted down, lowering the strap of her tank top. He nipped at her jaw, trailing kisses back up to her ear, telling her she was perfect.

She was everything. She was his.

How the hell could he have missed this? And how would they ever go back to the way it had been before?

Chapter Twelve

Gabby ran her hands over his chest, pushing him back so she could explore the defined muscles she hadn't expected him to have. He spent most of his days sitting in a chair, though he did use the treadmills in the complex's fitness center. She just hadn't let herself fully picture the reality of Owen shirtless. He was a real-life canvas and she wanted, *needed*, to leave her mark, before he realized there was no audience. *Which means this isn't for show.* Which meant, maybe, she had time to savor, but she couldn't quite convince herself to slow down.

When he'd stepped out of the closet, naked from the waist up, she'd lost the thread of their conversation. And now there was little talking, only hands gliding, words whispered, the rustle of his sheets as they twisted around the bed.

She was frenzied, scared of the moment ending. Everything ended, but not her and Owen. He moaned into the darkness when her lips found the sensitive spot where his shoulder met his neck. Even there, she felt his strength. He was hers—her strength and her rock. Her family. Her everything. And though it scared her, to let him feel what she felt, to show him, with her hands and her mouth and her gentle sighs, everything he meant to her, she couldn't hold back and she couldn't slow down. She knew life wasn't gentle about snatching things away, and if this was her one moment with him, she wanted everything she could get.

The furnace hummed in the quiet, a white-noise background against their pounding hearts. She felt his heartbeat, frantic, under her palm and pressed her lips to that spot, lingering until his hands threaded through her hair and pulled her up so they were kissing. Kissing Owen, *really* kissing him, was better than art. It was color and chaos wrapped together in calmness. It was breathtaking and beautiful. She didn't know one person could make her feel so much.

His lips were soft and warm and he tasted like toothpaste and desire. She couldn't touch enough of him at once. When her hands slid to the waistband of his pajama bottoms, his hand covered hers and the kissing stopped. Breathing heavily, she waited. Her pulse echoed in her ears.

Owen pulled her hand to his lips, kissing the knuckles with such gentleness. She felt his muscles tense and knew he was getting himself under control. Her heart caved in like crumpled paper. He was stopping them. Before they'd even started. Pain flared inside, a flash of light—quick and surprising. Then it seeped through her, pouring into her limbs. He didn't want her.

"Gabby."

Moments ago she'd cherished the sound of her name on his lips but now, in that same darkness, it was a slap in the face. She didn't want his excuses. His reasons. His Goddamn list of why this wasn't right. She pulled out of his arms and left the bed.

"Gabby, don't."

She laughed humorlessly. "Don't what? Go? Stay? Don't read into anything?"

He said nothing and all the warmth in the room, in her body, faded. She rubbed her hands up and down her arms, shuffling her feet on the softness of the carpet.

"I'm going to take a shower," she said. "We'll just pretend this didn't happen."

She didn't know exactly which "this" she was referring to—playing the part of his girlfriend, exposing her feelings, or making out like they'd been two people starving. Before she took her first step away from the bed, Owen was up, gripping her arms, yanking her close. His breathing was still uneven.

"No. You don't get to do that. You don't get to back away and close up," he said.

Gabby pulled at his grasp but he didn't let go. "You don't get to decide what I do."

He gave his own mirthless laugh. "I've never been so happy to have my family around."

"What?"

"You go shower if you need a minute because there's nowhere else to go. You can't run from this and you can't shut down because I needed five damn seconds to think."

Her voice rose. "Think about what?"

He shook her gently. "About *this*." He gestured back and forth between them with one hand. "About the fact that you drive me so crazy, I almost forgot my sister was sleeping down the hall. I want you, Gabby, and that changes things. It scares the hell out of me, but I'm not trying to pretend it didn't happen. I'll let you run and hide in the shower, but you need to let me have a few seconds to freak the hell out. And not be pissed because I did."

Despite his words and the clipped tone, she stopped shivering, stopped being cold. It was so perfectly Owen. Of course he would panic. It was a change to their regularly scheduled program. She stopped fighting him, let her hands relax on his chest. She was tired of fighting the feelings inside her, but they were better than going up against him. She didn't want tension between them. And the look on his face, the way his expression softened when she stepped closer, said he didn't want to fight either.

"I'm not pissed. Don't worry about it, Owen. Nothing has to change. I'm a big girl. I knew what I was signing on for."

He didn't let her go. His gaze burned into hers.

"Everything has already changed," he whispered.

She didn't want that. If she couldn't have *him* as the love of her life, she *needed* him to still be her best friend. Gabby pulled out of his grasp and wrapped her arms around her waist.

Would they be okay? They could still step back so they didn't wreck their friendship. She had to give him that out. "We can go back to the way it was."

His hand stroked her back and the touch sent tingles up her spine. "I don't want to. I didn't say I wanted to. It just kind of overwhelmed me for a minute. You, me. It's *us*. And my sister is sleeping on the couch. Like, footsteps away. Not exactly what I'd want for our first time."

God, even the thought of it filled her with so much longing she felt like she might burst. Everything he said made perfect sense, but fear still crept into her bones. "We can't wreck this. Us. What we have," she whispered.

His voice was strong and sure. "We won't. I just needed a minute. I couldn't breathe."

"That was the best part," she said.

His gaze swallowed her whole and he nodded his head slowly. "I know."

His lips touched hers again, softly, like a feather brushing over her. When he pulled back, he put his forehead to hers for a moment and closed his eyes. The unease settled inside Gabby as they breathed each other's air. The silence of the room surrounded them and her pulse stopped scrambling.

He set his chin on her head, tucking her into him in a way that made her feel safe. Loved. She could feel his heart racing still. He didn't like change and she'd never known anything but. She'd learned to face demons and move forward. There were some things in life you couldn't plan, couldn't predict or prepare for. Gabby had used the pain of that lesson to fuel her art and her life. Because she knew it only took one second for the world around you to become unrecognizable.

She pressed herself closer to Owen. Life could change in an instant, but right now, they were here. Together. Because they *both* wanted to be. And she'd be a fool to wreck it by wondering what if.

...

Waking up beside him after a night of sleeping in his arms, with even the possibility that they could try for real, that he might want to, was like looking through an unfiltered lens. Everything felt crisp and new. It was almost too much and Gabby's hands felt restless. She needed to paint. She needed to put her feelings about Owen's soft murmurings in the dark and keeping her close through the night onto paper. As she slipped from the bed, he moaned softly, pulling her back. Her heart actually fluttered. Waves of happiness rippled inside her and the feeling made her shaky.

"Go back to sleep," she whispered.

With barely any light, she sat in his chair, sketching him. She didn't need the light. The explosion of feelings inside her was bright enough to have the pen flying over the smooth texture of the page.

As she drew and shaded, her pulse settled, but her mind ignited. She turned the page, creating a series of five boxes. In one of them, she sketched the one painting she'd finished. The tiny heart lost in the storm of colorful emotions became larger in every picture, until the heart was at the forefront, the storm behind it. When she painted them, she'd have the color scheme go from dark to light. The heart in the final painting would all but pulsate with life and energy. If she could pull it off the way she saw it in her head.

"I love watching you work," Owen said, startling her with his raspy voice.

Her eyes wandered up the bed, taking in the way the sheet covered him, the way the fabric rose and fell with the shape of his body. She drank in his abdomen and the narrow trail of hair that led up, or down depending on which way she was traveling. She bit her lip, wishing he'd kicked free of the sheet in his sleep. By the time her eyes met his, he was watching her back, his gaze still sleepy, but amused.

Setting her book aside, she went to his side table and picked up his glasses, passing them to him. He took them with one hand and grabbed her wrist with the other, tugging her down on top of him.

"I don't even need them to know how you were looking at me. I could feel it."

She laughed and ducked her head into the crook of his neck, nuzzling there. His hands stroked her back, making her arch and sigh at the same time. His fingers played against her skin where her tank top rode up.

After they'd crawled back into the bed last night, they'd gone to sleep, wrapped in each other. Only clothes had separated them and when she'd awoken in the night, he'd still been holding her, like he didn't plan to let her go. If Owen needed time to adjust, it was the least she could give him. Seeing him sleep-tousled while his fingers slid over her skin tested her patience, but he was right: his family was there. Even though she wanted this, they both needed to accept that they'd crossed a threshold. Regardless of what they said, they'd never be able to go back to being 'just friends' in the way they had been. And that scared her almost as much as losing him completely.

"I told my family I'd take them back to the mall today,"

he said. She looked up, bringing her hand to the thin layer of stubble on his chin. It was rough under her fingers and she liked the sound of running her thumb back and forth. "Are you listening?"

"Family. Mall."

Owen laughed and squeezed her against him. "God, you're a distraction. I'm going to get up and make breakfast. If I don't show my mother I can cook, she'll never leave."

When someone knocked on the bedroom door, they both froze. Owen cringed when his mom's voice came through the wood. "Owen? Gabby? Are you up? I made breakfast. Merry Christmas Eve."

Owen pushed away from Gabby and pulled jeans out of his dresser, his movements hasty and almost frantic. "Okay, Mom. We don't need a wake-up call."

Gabby lay back on the bed, arching an eyebrow in amusement. His cool, sexy-calm was gone, and now it was like a scene from a rom-com. He jumped on one leg, trying to get into his jeans. When his eyes met Gabby's, they widened. She bit her lip.

"Someone is grumpy in the morning," Beth called.

She sat up, still holding back her laughter. "You can relax, Owen. It's your house. She can't ground you for making out with a girl in your bedroom," she whispered.

He was yanking a shirt out of the closet and turned to her with it in his hand. He took a deep breath and gave her a sheepish grin. "I know. I'm sorry. Just feels weird to be sitting half-naked on my bed with you and my mom at the door."

Gabby nodded, keeping her thoughts about how adorable he was to herself. She had things to do today and now that they were up, she needed to get started. "I'll grab my things and shower at my place."

Owen tossed the shirt beside her and pulled her up to standing. "What? Why? There's no reason for that. We'll get ready here, have breakfast, and go to the mall."

She liked that he didn't want her to leave, but since they'd spent every moment together so far, she hadn't even wrapped his gifts. A little space would do them both some good. He could spend some time with his family and she could get herself together so that just looking at him didn't make her want to strip him naked. She ran her hands over his chest again. Maybe she should try her hand at sculpting. "I'd like to paint a bit today, if there's time. Maybe I'll meet you guys at the mall, if that's okay? I also have a few errands to run and little things to pick up."

Owen sat down on the bed, pulling her between his legs. "What kinds of things?"

"Owen," his mother called through the door again. "Everything is ready."

Owen shook his head and stood up, grabbed his shirt and pulled it over his head. "Seriously?" He muttered it so only she could hear and then called back, "Okay, Mom."

Gabby laughed. "You'd better get out there. I'll be out in a minute."

He sighed, kissed the tip of her nose, and ran his hand down the length of her hair. Happiness settled deeply into Gabby's bones. When he left, she stayed in the same spot and closed her eyes, reliving the feeling of his breath on her face, his words in her ear, and his lips on hers. Since she was alone, she treated herself to a ten-second happy dance and then went to brush her teeth. This Christmas was already special because she was spending it with Owen and finally getting the family holiday she'd been craving. But the memory of Owen's touch brought it to a whole new level. She pushed aside the little voice that said it was too good to be true. She deserved this and so did Owen. Whatever happened, they'd always be friends. But the fact that she wasn't the only one who wanted more was the best Christmas present she could imagine.

Chapter Thirteen

Gabby finished up showering, enjoying the bit of quiet. Breakfast had been boisterous and fun. She liked listening to Owen's family talk. They moved from one topic to another without pause, making each other laugh. Dressing in jeans and a T-shirt, she tied her hair back. Owen's touches during breakfast had been more casual, less heated, which made sense. If he was feeling like her, it was better they not touch at all. Like the doughnuts again, once she took a bite…she wanted more. He'd tried to convince her to come to the mall with them again, but she'd held strong.

While she pulled gifts out of plastic bags, she tried not to worry about the fact that she'd gotten exactly what she wanted by being part of a lie. They'd work it out. Maybe if she could get him alone later, she could talk to him about coming clean.

Pulling out her phone, she selected a Christmas playlist. She'd been so worried that she didn't meet Owen's requirements for "dream girl." It troubled her she still didn't, but she reminded herself that wants could change and Owen definitely wanted her. It was obvious from his words. The way he touched her. The way his eyes darkened at her touch. She'd focus on that. On them. On trusting him to step outside his carefully created parameters and explore what had been lying there this whole time, waiting for him to notice.

"Enough. Have some faith," she told herself. She'd never had trouble believing in Owen before. She wouldn't start now. Turning up the volume on her docking station, she wrapped the box set of *Firefly* she'd bought for Owen. Next, she checked to see if the paint was dry on the sign she'd made for Owen's mom. She ran her fingers over the black script that read *Family Is Everything*. She'd stenciled it onto three pieces of a palette she'd connected at the back. After painting it a cheery yellow, she'd added the words and then the stain. One thing about staying at Owen's, she was able to spread her work out and move from one project to the next without worrying about space.

She wasn't sure what would happen between them, but unlike Owen, she could handle the not knowing. For a while. Certainly until they got through Christmas with his family. Despite Owen's reluctance to spend holidays with them, Gabby loved having them around. They were lively and funny. A different side of Owen was revealed in their presence. They laughed constantly and loved without restraint, and it was difficult not to want to be part of that. Even if she'd tried to shrink back from it, they would have pulled her into the fold. It was just how they were. And she loved it.

So, enjoy it. Once they went home, she and Owen could go back to their own spaces and figure out where they stood.

Gabby refused to let a little thing like being hopelessly in love with him ruin their friendship or rush him into declaring his own feelings.

She heard the knock at her door only because the music had quieted to switch songs. Looking through the peephole was more habit than worry, but in light of recent events, it was also smart.

"What's up, Jake?" She wasn't in the mood for him. His eyes were bloodshot and his clothes were more rumpled than usual.

Tunneling a hand through his hair, he cast a quick glance around. "Hey. There are a couple of officers in the multipurpose room. They told me to gather everyone, but it's a pain in the ass. I gotta knock on every damn door. Since they're the ones who want to interview every damn tenant, you'd think they could go door to door themselves. Can you help me?"

Gabby bit back her smile. There were four floors in the building, but only three held apartments. She was betting Jake had come to her first, which meant there was no reason for him to look like he'd climbed Everest.

"Sure." It was Christmas. She could be generous. And it would get her out of her own head. Or heart. Or both.

"Yeah? Okay, I'll go back to the lobby and you start gathering them."

He turned and walked away, leaving Gabby with her mouth hanging open. Collecting herself before he stepped onto the elevator, she called out, "That's more like doing it for you than helping."

He gave her a creepy half grin then turned as the doors slid open. "You're a doll," he said as they closed.

Gabby huffed out a sigh. More like an idiot. She quickly texted Brady, asking him to knock on the doors on the second floor, since he lived there. She grabbed her phone and wallet and shoved them in her back pocket, made sure she had her keys in case she didn't come back later, and headed out to start her floor. She finished hers easily enough, since Owen was out with his family. When she went down to the third floor, three neighbors didn't answer, and two were heading down now. She knocked on the final door on the third floor, a corner unit like Owen's. Not-so-Neighborly-Wyatt yanked it open, his scowl fully intact.

"What?" His dark hair stuck out at odd angles.

Really? She put her hands on her hips. "Why are you so grumpy?" She didn't need to know, but she was curious.

His eyes widened. "Are you joking? You did not knock on my door to ask me that."

Gabby took a step back, mildly amused but not stupid. Clearly, he didn't want to open up to her. "No. I came to tell you that the police are interviewing all the tenants downstairs. Your charming presence has been requested, along with everyone else."

She turned, neighborly duty complete, and stalked toward the elevator. *Men.*

She gave a small gasp when she stepped onto the elevator and Wyatt stepped in with her. He seemed bigger in the small space. He was wearing jeans and a pullover hoody that read *Boston Strong*. He definitely didn't dress like a mobster.

"You should wear a bell," Gabby said. She gripped the railing that went around three-quarters of the elevator. It occurred to her whoever was breaking into things could very well be dangerous.

"Excuse me?"

Gabby stared at him, waiting for her instincts to speak up and tell her she should fear this man. But they didn't. He looked more exasperated than deadly.

"You're too quiet. I didn't hear you close your door or come down the hallway after me."

"Maybe I should just keep up a constant stream of chatter, like you."

Were his lips twitching? "It's not a bad idea. But the bell would work, too."

He shook his head and gestured for her to go first when

the elevator doors opened to the lobby. Gabby recognized many of the people milling about, but not all of them. In one room, like this, it felt like a lot more than eighteen apartments.

He crossed his arms beside her. "And I'm not grumpy. Old men are grumpy."

"I'm sorry, how does that support your argument? Because from my side, it sounds like you just confirmed your grumpiness *and* called yourself old."

This time, his smile was hard to miss. It changed his face, brightening his eyes, and, ironically, made him look younger. Definitely more approachable.

"Careful. Someone might see you with that smile on your face," Gabby said.

"Do you ever shut up?"

For some reason, his dry tone made it impossible for her to feel insulted. She shrugged. "Rarely."

He started to respond but then his smile faded and his body tensed. He took a step closer to her when a hand gripped her wrist. She turned, just as he did, and saw it was Owen. Wyatt didn't seem to care and his eyes zeroed in on the spot where Owen held her arm.

Owen met his gaze, arched an eyebrow, and stepped closer to Gabby. "Hey, babe." He kissed her cheek, but his body stayed angled toward their neighbor. Wyatt's glare softened before he gave a chin nod and walked away. Their other neighbors chatted nosily around them, but Gabby focused only on Owen. His eyes were a little wild and his dark hair was falling onto his forehead. She brushed it back, her fingers tingling with the urge to play with the dark strands.

Her belly tumbled just at the sight of him. "Hey." Her voice was too breathy.

"Hi. What's going on?" He looked around, waved at someone, and then pulled Gabby over to the side. There was nowhere to sit. Three uniformed officers were asking a series of questions, jotting down answers and sending people away. It was busy, but fairly organized. Jake was pacing the small area of carpet near the door, rubbing the back of his neck.

"They're asking questions," Gabby clarified. "Jake said it shouldn't take long. I think they're going by unit number. They told him it was easier than knocking on every door, which he didn't seem to agree with, seeing as it meant *he* had to."

"Okay. Gabs, about this morning…about my freaking out when my mom came to the door," Owen said. He lowered his forehead to hers. His glasses felt like a barrier.

She shook her head. "It's okay. Everything is fine. We'll figure things out after your family leaves."

The corners of his eyes crinkled the way they did when he was working out a problem. "I don't want you to think—"

"Unit 403," one of the uniforms called.

"That's you. I'll meet you upstairs when I'm done, okay?" Gabby kissed his cheek and gave him a little shove when he hesitated. He looked back at her once before he reached the table, where he spoke with an older, burlier cop.

Mrs. Haverman was talking about her cats, loudly, to the youngest looking officer, who was trying to hurry her up.

"Just answer the question, ma'am," he said.

Gabby leaned against the wall, watching her neighbors. People were grumbling about their holiday plans being interrupted, but it was better than having the cops show up on Christmas Day. It was hard to believe it was tomorrow. His parents were leaving a few days after Christmas, and she couldn't help thinking about what would happen when they were alone. She'd thought Owen would have to tell his family, by phone of course, that they'd broken up. All pretending done. But maybe now, he wouldn't have to. She hated lying, but was it different when that lie became the truth? *Definitely a gray area.* Gabby pushed off the wall, startled when Owen returned only a moment later.

"That was fast."

Owen took her hand, linking their fingers in a way that was becoming routine. He looked down at their hands, then met her gaze.

"Not much to say. They have our names and apartments. Nothing of mine was stolen or broken, so I'm not much help. I'll wait for you."

Before Gabby could tell him she still needed to finish up some things, she heard Owen's mother calling his name from the other end of the crowd.

Beth smiled, her eyes crinkling at the corners. "Hi Gabby. Owen, honey. I forgot something in your truck. Is Gabby okay with us just ordering in tonight?"

"Sounds good," Gabby said. Though, the home cooked-mom meals were pretty fantastic.

"I hadn't asked her yet, but I had a feeling she'd be fine with it," Owen said, bumping her hip with his. She grinned at him.

He knew her better than anyone. Did he know this wasn't just physical attraction for her? Could he see it? Feel how much she loved him? Owen squeezed her hand and when he looked at her, his brows were furrowed together. "Are you okay?"

"Oh, I hope you're not coming down with something," Beth said, stepping closer.

"I'm fine. I'm totally fine," Gabby said. Owen didn't look convinced. He pulled her a bit closer, leaned down so his lips were at her ear.

"We need to talk," he said.

Gabby shivered. When his lips brushed her ear like that, talking wasn't the first thing that came to mind.

"Owen, honey. Your truck?"

Owen's growl vibrated against Gabby's skin. "How does she always manage to interrupt at the worst time?"

Gabby went up on tiptoe and kissed his cheek. "She's a mom. I think it's part of the training. I'll meet you upstairs."

Owen stepped back, and his eyes were shadowed in a way that made Gabby's heart squeeze. "Sorry, Mom. Let's go get your stuff." He rubbed Gabby's shoulder. "We'll talk later."

Gabby was called up by one of the officers a few minutes after Owen and his mom left. He was kind and routine, making it easy to answer the questions.

"Did someone mention the mailboxes to you?" she asked when they were finishing up.

The officer looked down at some sheets of paper in front of him. "Hmm. We're collecting information on the storage room damage and thefts. Was your mailbox broken into?"

"No. But someone tried."

He made a note and promised to speak with the other officers. When she made her way to the elevators, Jake stopped her with a hand on her arm. She looked down at it with a hard frown and back up at him. He removed his hand.

"What'd they ask you?" *What is his problem?*

"Probably the same things they asked you," Gabby snapped.

Wyatt caught her eye and started heading in her direction. When Jake noticed, he mumbled something and stalked away. The other neighbor stopped walking toward her and just stared for a moment before his eyes trailed Jake. She couldn't think about whatever was happening right now. Gabby's mind and heart were jumping around for joy, and it was starting to make her dizzy. As if the holiday wasn't thrilling enough, she was pretty certain Owen was going to give her the best gift she could ever imagine: him. With him came family. Talk about icing on the proverbial cake.

When she made it back to the apartment, the TV was blaring clear into the hallway. Leo was sprawled on the couch, watching sports highlights.

"Hey there, Gabby. You missed out on mini doughnuts at the mall," he said.

"She wouldn't have if you hadn't eaten the ones we brought back for her," Patty said. Owen's family liked to eat almost as much as she did. One more thing to love about them.

"No worries. Once I have one, I can't stop. It can get a little dangerous. Where's everyone else?"

Leo turned the volume down on the TV. "Lia's in the shower, and Beth went to get something out of Owen's truck. We're going to order in. Owen says there's a little Italian place around the corner that you guys love."

Love. The word was trapped in her brain. God, she was becoming a ball of sap. "Yes, it's great. Okay. I'm going to go back to my place. I have a few things I need to bring over and put under the tree."

Leo waved and turned back to the TV. The door was slightly open, making her pause and frown. She'd shut it when she left with Jake, hadn't she? Pushing it open enough to slip inside, she heard voices. Her heart nearly leapt out of her chest when she realized they were coming from the living room. She was frozen, one hand on the door, her body half in the hall, half in her home. When she recognized Owen's voice, she sighed in relief. *Way to spook yourself.* She heard Beth's voice as well. *Argh.* She hadn't covered the present. She started toward the living room, hoping Beth hadn't seen the sign.

"I want you to give it to her. When you said she was the one, I took it out of the safe," Beth said.

Gabby froze. She didn't even breathe. Standing in the hallway, she listened to their conversation.

She slapped a hand silently to her mouth at Beth's next words: "It's Grandma Shelly's engagement ring."

Dots danced in front of Gabby's eyes. She'd tried to play

it cool, but maybe Owen did know exactly how she felt. And maybe he felt the same way. Maybe what Owen meant by "we need to talk" was code for "hey, did you know I'm totally head over heels in love with you, too?" She just wanted the chance to see where they could go. She wasn't thinking marriage. At least not right this minute. But it'd be another lie to say she'd never imagined spending her life with him. It had worried her to think he didn't want kids, but now she knew she'd been wrong there, too. She'd been tying her hopes around the idea that they could try a real relationship. The idea of so much more was a balloon expanding in her chest. *Oh my God...*

"Uh…Mom, I don't want to give Gabby that." She could hear in the pitch of his voice that he was trying to be polite.

The balloon popped, painfully, sending arrows of pain at her heart. Of course not. It was too soon. One heavy make-out session did not equate a proposal. They hadn't even been on a real date, so his answer was logical. Why did logic hurt so badly?

"Owen, it's a family ring. It's beautiful."

Gabby knew from his tone, he was tamping down on irritation. "Drop it, Mom. Come on, let's get back."

Gabby inched her way toward the door, holding her breath. She needed to go. She didn't need to hear this. She wasn't meant to hear this.

"No, I will not drop it. You love that girl; I can see it. And she loves you. Now take the ring."

She had her hand on the doorknob when her stomach dropped out from under her.

"Mom, knock it off, please. I don't need your help with my relationships and there's no chance in hell I would give Gabby the ring. Now drop it. Please."

Gabby's vision blurred but she managed to get the door open soundlessly. Not waiting for it to shut behind her, she moved down the hallway as quick as her unsteady feet would take her. She couldn't breathe. She was trying, but the air wouldn't fill her lungs. She pushed open the door to the stairwell, welcoming the cooler air. Cement stairs went up one way and down the other. Gabby collapsed onto the closest one. *Stop. Stop panicking. It means nothing.* She wouldn't let a conversation she wasn't meant to hear rip her apart. She might be the artsy one, but it didn't mean she couldn't apply logic to a situation. *Which means not jumping to conclusions.* Still, her eyes burned like she might cry. *No crying. Don't wreck this.* They couldn't wreck it. They'd promised. She needed to get herself together. She couldn't do this now. Another door opened and closed and footsteps echoed around her. *Please don't be Owen. Please.*

Wyatt was taking two stairs at a time. When he rounded the stair rail, he stopped, looked down at Gabby, and his lips tilted farther down.

"What's wrong with you?" he asked.

Gabby huffed out a far-from-humorous laugh. "A lot, apparently. Nothing for you to be concerned about. Weren't you just in the lobby with everyone else?" She blinked away the wetness in her eyes.

"Weren't you?"

Gabby shook her head. "Never mind." She stood, and even on the step, she was barely eye level with him.

His mouth shifted into a flat line. For him, it was almost a smile. "Are you okay?"

Gabby parted her lips, surprised by the softness of his voice. Instead of answering, she just nodded.

"Then why are you sitting in a stairwell crying?"

Because I'm an idiot. No. Don't think like that. If she let go of her hope, she'd lose it. She'd curl into a ball and drown herself in tears. Straightening her shoulders, she replied, "I'm not crying," before another thought occurred to her, making her throat tighten. "Why are *you* in the stairwell?"

He pursed his lips. "Exercise," he said.

Gabby rolled her eyes. "Right. Me too. I have to go… somewhere." *Anywhere but here.*

She'd taken a step away when he said her name. It sounded foreign coming from his lips.

He turned, gave her another almost smile. "If you need someone to kick your boyfriend's ass, I could arrange it."

She couldn't decide if the offer was sweet or scary. "Not this time," she said and turned to go just in case the tears wanted to make an appearance in front of her always-grumpy-sometimes-sweet-possibly-mob-connected neighbor.

I'll be okay… It'll be okay.

Hurrying down the stairs, she tried to think of what she could do to give herself time to reattach her game face. Continuing down until she reached the basement, she exited the stairwell and leaned against the wall. She wouldn't assume the worst; she could control that. Her breathing, however, took more effort to get a grip on. *You get five minutes and then you pull yourself together. It's Christmas. It'll be okay.* She wished with everything in her that she wasn't telling herself another lie.

Chapter Fourteen

"Well, there's absolutely no reason to be rude, Owen. I'm still your mother," Beth said.

Her tone made him cringe. He'd just gotten his head wrapped around the fact that he wanted to see Gabriella Michaelson naked—really soon—and now his mom was pushing his grandma's ugly-ass ring on him. Talk about Mach speed. Though, oddly enough, the thought of giving Gabby a ring didn't seem as crazy as it would have even a week ago. He tried to rein in his ping-ponging thoughts.

"I'm sorry. Look, I appreciate the gesture, I really do. But that ring isn't for Gabby. She's unique and different and she should have a ring that reflects that. Besides," he said, lowering his voice, "Grandma Shelly was married four times. Her first engagement ring doesn't exactly inspire confidence." He really shouldn't have lied to them. Now he was leading his mother to believe he planned to propose with a different ring and he hadn't even spoken his feelings out loud yet. To himself or to Gabby. She was right: one lie led to another.

His mother started to argue, but really, what could she

say? She stared at the simple diamond ring and then slipped it into her pocket with a sigh.

"Fine. But I still think it would be nice to give it to her on Christmas morning. You could always tell her it's a place holder until you get the one you imagined for her," Beth suggested.

Owen couldn't put into words, not to his mother, what he imagined with Gabby. He'd always imagined her in his future, but now he was beginning to feel like she *was* his future. He'd already dug himself a ditch of half-truths and Gabby deserved more. He needed to tell her that he wanted what they were pretending to be the real thing, to see where they could take things. Life was too short and he didn't want to waste it. He'd already done too much of that.

Standing this close to his mom, he could see the signs of her aging, and it reminded him that he spent too much time worrying about things that just didn't matter. He'd avoided his family this Christmas because it meant a few days of craziness. He'd do better. He'd change. If he was going to ask Gabby to accept the harder parts of him, he could…but she didn't want him to change. She wanted him as he was. Still, it didn't mean he couldn't adjust, starting with setting things right. How could he ask for more and tell her how he felt when what he'd asked of her this week went against something that mattered so much to her: honesty.

"Come on," Owen said, impatient to be with Gabby.

"What about my idea for Christmas morning?"

He sighed. "What about it?"

His mom gave him another don't-you-use-that-tone look. "It's a good idea, and you've left us out of enough things in your life. Why can't we watch?"

Guilt tugged at the corners of his heart. Why the hell *had* he left them out of so much?

"We won't say a word. We'll just watch and then celebrate

with you," Beth said, squeezing her hands together.

Right. Because they don't believe in breathing room. Though maybe he'd given himself too much space. It was unfair to them, and he was missing out on moments he'd never get back, moments Gabby would do anything to have with her own family. It was one more thing he could give her.

Owen pulled his mom into a hug. She wanted what was best for him. "Mom. I love you, but you have to let me do this my way. I'm not proposing to Gabby in front of you guys. It isn't her and, quite honestly, it isn't me." He couldn't imagine declaring his feelings in front of people. Not that he was ashamed of them—hell, he kind of wanted to shout them out, but there was something intimate and genuine about quietly sharing his feelings with Gabby. Just the two of them.

His mom sniffled and his stomach twisted. He didn't want the women in his life to cry because of him. "Well, don't wait forever to do it," she said. "I'd like to actually be able to hold some grandbabies before my arms are too frail to stand the weight."

Owen chuckled. If he didn't have to live with the drama, it was a bit easier to make light of it. He guided his mom toward the door, which was ajar. Owen stared at it for a second before answering her. "You know, Ophelia is older than me. It seems like you should be nagging her."

His mother swatted him on the arm as she walked past him. Inside his apartment, Ophelia was helping Aunt Patty at the table while his dad argued with the TV.

"Hey. Where's Gabby?"

His dad didn't look up. "She's with you."

Owen waited. His dad looked over at him. "Isn't she with you?"

"No. This is your wife. Not Gabby."

His mom swatted him again. "Don't smart-mouth your dad. He's still—"

"My father. Right. Sorry. Seriously, where's Gabby?"

"She went over to her apartment about ten minutes ago. No way could you have missed her," Patty said. She rolled cookies out on his dining room table and the scent of ginger and cinnamon flavored the air.

Unease tickled the back of Owen's neck. Gabby wasn't at her place. There actually was no way he could have missed her...if she'd come all the way in. If she hadn't; if she'd only come part way in and left in a hurry, the door might not have closed behind her, which would have left it open just a bit... Like it had been.

"Shit."

Beth *tsked*. "Language, Owen."

"What's wrong?" Ophelia asked. She twisted her hair up as she spoke and walked over to him. "You okay? You're pale."

"Gabby came over to her apartment?"

"Didn't Aunt Patty just tell you that? I was in the shower."

"What's the matter, Owen?" His mother was stowing the ring back in her purse.

"If Gabby came to the apartment and we didn't hear her, she heard us talking about the ring."

"What? What ring?" Ophelia's voice rose into an octave that made Owen's ears burn.

"You're proposing?" Patty squealed.

His dad laughed and pulled himself up off the couch. "Well, way to go, son. Gotta say, I wondered if you'd ever make it happen, but I see why you waited. One heck of a girl you've got yourself. Definitely worth the wait."

Owen's stomach heaved. "No. Stop. I'm not proposing. This isn't... no. No. I have to find Gabby. Order dinner. There's a take-out menu on the fridge. Eat without me."

He didn't wait for them to say anything more, but he heard them asking questions as he grabbed his keys and wallet and headed out the door. She wasn't at her place. Where would she go?

His heart worked overtime as he waited for the elevator, and when it didn't come fast enough, he took the stairs. He was reaching the second floor, his feet racing down the steps, when he heard angry voices. Coming to a halt, he saw the rough-looking, always-scowling neighbor he didn't want Gabby anywhere near. Wyatt. She'd said his name was Wyatt. He was holding Jake against the wall by the collar of his shirt. Jake's face was white and his hands gripped the arms of the bigger man.

"If I find out it was you, I will personally kick the crap out of you. Got that?" His moody neighbor chose that moment to shove Jake and turn around. He didn't look sorry, or particularly pleased, when he saw Owen.

"Everything okay here, guys?" Owen clenched his fists. He didn't need this right now. His keys dug into the palm of his hand.

"Just fine. As long as our apartment manager keeps his hands off people's belongings, everything will stay that way."

Owen glared at Jake, putting two and two together. "Seriously, man? You're the one who broke into the mailboxes and the storage room?"

Jake straightened his T-shirt and made a show of smoothing it out. He sneered. "I didn't actually get into the mailboxes. Someone took something of mine. Someone in this building. Don't see why I can't find out who."

Wyatt nearly growled. "For one thing, you moron, it's a goddamn federal offense to tamper with mailboxes."

Owen looked back and forth between them. "He's right. And besides that, what the hell is next? You can't find what you're looking for, you going to break into our homes next?"

"No!" Jake had the gall to look offended.

"No. He's not. Because he's going to give his resignation

or I'm going to turn him in to the cops."

Jake's eyes widened and sounds, but no words, sputtered from his mouth.

His neighbor wasn't friendly and he seemed to have his eyes on Gabby way too often for Owen's taste, but he'd just scored some major points. Owen stuck out his hand. "Owen."

Moody eyed his hand before sighing and shaking Owen's. "Wyatt."

"Nice to meet you. I think."

Wyatt shrugged. "Fair enough."

"Dude, you aren't serious, are you?" Jake wasn't just pale now, he was almost translucent.

Wyatt straightened his shoulders and took a step toward him. "You have until the day after Christmas to give your notice or I *will* tell the cops it was you and you *will* be charged. At the least, you'll be fined, but I'll see to it that you get locked up. Especially if I can prove what it was I think you were looking for."

Jake shrunk back. "What about until then?"

Wyatt put his hands on his hips and arched an eyebrow at Jake. "You're stupid, but I'm guessing you're not stupid enough to try anything in that time?"

"Whatever, man. I hate this building anyway. Goddamn waste of my time and talent."

Jake threw open the door leading to the hallway and went through it. Owen looked back at Wyatt, who stood a couple inches taller than him.

"How can you be so sure the cops will take your word for it?"

"Let's just say I have friends in high places," Wyatt said. "Speaking of friends, you should encourage your girlfriend to pick better ones than that douche. She's too nice to everyone."

"Jesus. Gabby. I need to find Gabby," Owen said, nearly jolting forward. He hated the thought of her feelings being hurt. Why had she run? Why not just talk to him? He tried to remember exactly what he'd said.

Wyatt's body language changed, became more alert. "You the reason she was sitting on the stairs in tears?"

Owen's stomach dropped like a cable car cut loose. "You saw her? Wait. She was crying?" He'd made her cry. His gut cramped. He was supposed to dry her tears, not cause them.

Wyatt nodded, giving nothing away with the hard glare of his eyes or the deep frown he always wore. "About fifteen minutes ago. You screw up?"

Owen didn't answer because he wasn't entirely sure, so Wyatt continued, casually, like they were talking about the Red Sox. "Told her I'd kick your ass if she needed."

"If I don't clear things up, I might just let you," Owen said. If he didn't fix things with Gabby, nothing would hurt in comparison.

Wyatt's arms flexed when he crossed them over his wide chest. Owen winced. *Almost nothing.* "She took the stairs down," Wyatt said.

Owen stared at him a moment longer, then nodded. "Thanks." He didn't wait for a reply but took off down the stairs, intent on reaching the parking garage and his truck. He flung the final door open and almost rammed right into her. She was holding rolls of wrapping paper. Her eyes were shiny, but no tears marred her cheeks. His heart raced like he'd been running up the stairs instead of down.

"Owen," she said, her step halting. Blinking at him, she stayed rooted to a spot in the dim hallway that felt entirely too far away. He closed the distance between them and crushed her against his chest.

"I thought you'd left," he said against her hair.

She shifted, the wrapping paper crinkling between them. "Where would I go?" He hoped he was imagining the tinge of sadness in her tone. He wanted to give her happiness. Always.

Which meant he needed to fix things and make them right.

Pushing away from him, she gave a small laugh that sounded nothing like the one that made his blood rush. "What are you doing down here?" she asked.

"Looking for you. My dad said you'd gone over to your place," Owen replied. He shoved his hands in his pockets to keep from dragging her close again. He needed to know how bad the damage was before he could start unraveling it and piecing them back together. He'd never get over it if he ruined things between them.

"I did, but I heard your voice. And your mom's. Sounded like you were arguing and I didn't want to interrupt." She held up the wrapping paper. "And I needed more of this."

She didn't blink and he wondered if maybe she hadn't heard. "Arguing?" He waited to see if she'd elaborate.

Gabby shrugged. "Yeah. Sounded like it. You seemed frustrated. Is everything okay?"

Owen studied Gabby and thought of how precious she was to him. Looking at her now, he realized she was like air to him. Necessary. Without her, he literally wouldn't be able to breathe. "Everything is fine. You're sure you didn't overhear anything?"

Another weak laugh and her eyes went to the carpet. "No." She looked up, met his gaze. "Was there something you didn't want me to hear?"

Owen's heart felt like it was pumping too hard. "My mom was just being pushy. I worried maybe you overheard and I didn't want you to misunderstand."

Like a veil coming over her features, she hid her thoughts from him. He hated when he couldn't read her face. If she were mad, he'd apologize. Hurt, he'd beg forgiveness. He just needed to know what to do.

She stepped around him, started for the stairs. "Your parents love you. What you see as pushy might be them wanting to be part of your life. Let them in a little and maybe they'll surprise you."

He followed behind her and her words sunk in. Let them in. He needed to tell them the truth. That was the only way to really start a life with Gabby. When they reached the first landing, he put a hand on her arm. Unable to resist, he leaned down and kissed her, nearly sighing in relief when her mouth opened under his.

Pulling back, he tucked a curl behind her ear. The desire to be with her, to hold her close, to breathe only air they shared was almost overwhelming. Humbling. "Gabby. I would never hurt you. Not for anything." But was that a lie, too? Because he already had. She said she hadn't overheard, but something was wrong. Not for a second did he believe she'd lie to him about something important. Or anything at all. But what else could it be? He felt it and he could see it. He knew her. If she hadn't overheard, then it had to be the lying. It was taking its toll. This was a hard time of year for her anyway, and he'd compounded it by asking so much of her. But what if he hadn't? He would have missed all this. That made it hard to regret entirely, but that didn't mean he couldn't right a wrong.

"I know," she whispered, her voice pulling him out of his thoughts.

"I need you to know how much you matter to me. It's one thing to say it, but I think I need to show you. If you'll give me a chance?"

Her eyes burned with emotion, and he hated not knowing if it was happy or sad. With the rolls of paper clutched in one arm, she gripped his shirt with her other hand. "I'm giving you a chance. I'm giving us a chance. You matter to me, too. You don't know how much."

He did. He knew how much because he felt it, too. But it wasn't fair to tell her now when his family was upstairs waiting on them, worrying about them. He'd clear things up, and then when they were alone, he'd tell her the truth he might never have realized if they hadn't started down this path.

"I know," he said. She met his gaze and then turned to go up the stairs. He took her hand and walked with her, letting the quiet soothe the still rapid pace of his heart. He'd fix it. He hadn't been fair to the people he loved most.

As they approached his apartment, he stopped her once more.

He lowered his mouth, tracing over her lips with his tongue, hearing her sigh as she leaned into him, pressed her lips against his. When he felt like he was seconds away from not being able to let her go, he pulled back.

"You deserve so much," he whispered.

She gave a laugh that he couldn't decipher. Maybe part humor, part heartache?

"All I want is you," she said. And his heart actually leapt at the words.

"Then let's go in and celebrate Christmas. For real."

Chapter Fifteen

Gabby opened one eye and peeked at the clock. Five fifteen. Only ten minutes had passed since she'd last checked. She was being ridiculous, but she couldn't fall back asleep. Owen's deep, even breaths filled the silence. She rolled to her other side and put a hand on his chest, focusing on the rise and fall as she willed herself to go back to sleep until a reasonable, adult-like hour arrived.

Owen had been so serious the night before. She wanted to believe everything would be okay. She'd gone against her own rules and lied about overhearing him, because she hadn't been ready to have him say, face to face, that she wasn't his idea of forever. So she'd pushed down her feelings, lied, and decided that if this was all she was getting, this time with him and his family, she was taking it. He was her best friend and he deserved a little faith. She wouldn't let words out of context wreck their Christmas or destroy what she felt. No way was she imagining the feelings between them.

In her heart, she hoped by "fix it," he meant he'd tell her he loved her or, at least, could love her the way she loved him. She couldn't think of what else he could mean by fixing everything and had slept restlessly wondering.

At six twenty, she opened both eyes. *What was that?* She nudged Owen's shoulder and heard it again. A soft knock.

"Owen," she whispered, leaning up and putting her face close to his. She shook his shoulder. Another knock. Owen's eyes popped open and he flinched comically, his eyes flaring wide.

"What? What's wrong?"

Gabby laughed. Everything else could wait. She wanted her family Christmas. "Nothing. It's Christmas."

This time when the knock came, she wasn't the only one to hear it. Owen glared at the door. "Ophelia, are you seriously waking us up?" he said, sitting up to look at the clock. "At six thirty in the morning?"

Excitement stirred in Gabby's stomach. She threw back the covers as Ophelia spoke through the door.

"It kind of sounds like you're already awake, so technically, no."

Gabby giggled and opened the door. Ophelia stood in her PJs, her hands clasped together under her chin.

"Merry Christmas," Gabby said.

Ophelia threw her arms around Gabby and rocked back and forth. "Merry Christmas. Get up, Owen. I already put on coffee. Santa was here."

When Lia took off down the hallway, Gabby turned to see Owen getting out of the bed.

"Santa?"

Owen's sleepy eyes perked up. "You'll see," was all he said. "Wait for me, okay?" He walked into the en-suite and Gabby did as he asked.

When was the last time you were up this early on Christmas morning? Gabby's memories of her last holiday with her parents had faded like a worn photograph. They'd loved getting up early. Often, her father had woken her long before dawn. Since their passing, she'd grown out of the habit. She'd spent a few years with friends, and a few alone. She hadn't felt this type of anticipation toward the morning in a very long time.

Owen came out of the bathroom and smiled at her, took her hand, and they followed the cheery sound of his family waiting in the living room. The smell of coffee and cinnamon greeted them. Gabby saw fresh cinnamon buns sitting on the counter, but before she could comment, she was enveloped in a warm hug.

"Merry Christmas, Gabby. We're so happy to share it with you," Beth said, then released her to hug Owen. "Good morning, sweetheart."

Leo gave her a side-hug and Patty kissed her cheek. Gabby took it all in as coffee was poured and delicious looking cinnamon buns were passed around. Music played softly in the background and the lights of the tree flickered perfectly. Outside, it was still dark, but someone had pulled open the window shades.

Gabby's breath caught in her lungs when she noticed the red stockings—six of them—lying on the hearth of the fireplace, full to the brim. One of them had her name written across the top. She closed her eyes, tried to stop the tears from surfacing. Owen came to her side, passing her a cup of coffee.

In a low voice that only she could hear, he asked, "You okay?"

Gabby nodded, not trusting the words to come without tears. Owen slipped an arm around her shoulder, pulling her against his side.

"See?" he whispered. "Santa came."

She sipped her coffee, hoping it would help loosen the lump in her throat. A few tears escaped, but when Owen started to comment, she just shook her head and wiped them away. How could she explain how perfect this moment felt?

She had a family. *Hopefully for good.* Nerves swirled inside her like she'd gone over a bump too fast. *Enjoy the moment.*

"Let the girl sit down, son," Leo said, moving over on the couch. Ophelia sat with her aunt on the love seat. Owen sat beside Gabby and Beth handed out stockings. When she gave Gabby hers, their eyes met.

"Thank you for this," Gabby said, her throat still uncomfortably tight.

Beth smiled, her own eyes watery. "Oh, honey. It was absolutely my pleasure. I look forward to spending so many Christmases with you."

Then she passed Owen his and ruffled his hair. "You see that, dear? Gabby likes Christmas with us. So next year we'll have a bit more space when you two come home to celebrate."

Gabby beamed at Owen. His eyes, which he kept on Gabby's, were smiling when he answered. "We'll be there, Mom." *He's committing to next year. It's really happening.* She didn't know exactly what "it" was, but she had a feeling that, in front of his family, Owen was going to spell out his true feelings. She'd thought he'd want to tell her in private for the first time, but maybe he'd taken her advice to let them in.

When everyone had their stockings in front of them, they dove in. Gabby laughed at the trinkets Beth had found. Tiny soaps and shampoos, chocolates, and a Christmas ornament.

The smell of the cinnamon buns was driving her mad so she took a break to have a bite. "Mmm. When did you make these?"

"We made them last night after all you sleepy heads turned in for the night," Patty said, grinning as she held up candy cane earrings. "Beth, where do you find these things? You are absolutely the best stocking stuffer."

"Thank you. It's one of my favorite things to do," Beth

said. Leo leaned over to kiss his wife's cheek.

They nibbled and laughed and shared stories. The fire glowed and made the room comfortably warm. Gabby tried to latch on to each moment, to file it away. It was like this one morning had healed an aching part of her soul that had gone missing twelve years ago. Nothing could replace her family, but knowing she was no longer alone was a gift she couldn't fathom.

Owen passed her a box with her name on it. "You doing all right?"

"I am. I'm wonderful," she said.

He pressed a gentle kiss to her mouth, then leaned back. "I already knew that."

Gabby just smirked at him and mouthed the word "dork." He tugged a lock of her hair playfully, then nudged the present on her lap.

"Open it," he said.

Peeling the wrap off without restraint, she found a gorgeous five-by-seven wooden frame nestled inside. The wood was purposely worn to make it look older, and the black and white picture of her and Owen smiling made Gabby's heart burst open, like there was too much love and joy inside her to contain. She turned, wrapped her arms around Owen's neck, and hugged him tight. Tears streamed down her cheeks and she couldn't hold them back. Owen's arms held her strong.

"Hey. You okay?"

She nodded into the crook of his neck, then pulled back. Everyone was eyeing her somewhat warily, like they didn't want to further upset her. But she wasn't upset.

"You are all the greatest people. This has been the best Christmas I can remember in so long. Thank you for making me feel so included." She sniffed as she wiped at her tears.

Owen's arm pulled her close and she leaned her head against him.

"You'll always be included, Gabriella. You're part of our family now, and if Owen does something to mess this up, you just leave him home and come spend next Christmas with us. He doesn't even know the words to most of the carols, anyway," Beth said.

Everyone laughed, including Owen. "Thanks, Mom. Way to sell me out."

The morning was nothing short of perfect. Min called shortly before they were ready to eat—apparently Owen's family ate their "dinner" in the early afternoon. Owen had pointed out she'd like this because it meant being able to snack on the leftovers later in the day and through the evening. As they waited for Patty and Beth to finish up the side dishes, Gabby grew antsy to see what Owen meant by fixing things. Thinking to get her mind off of things, she'd offered to help in the kitchen, but Patty had said she needed her own distraction and Beth had told her to just enjoy relaxing, which was more difficult than it sounded. She'd sort of expected something— she didn't know what—to have happened by now. Until he said otherwise, she wouldn't poke holes in her chance for happiness. She excused herself from the room and answered the call.

"Merry Christmas," Min said when Gabby answered.

"To you, too. How are you? I can hear everyone in the background," Gabby said.

"Ha, that's barely half of them. I'm good. We've already eaten enough for a week and there's still dinner to make."

"Owen's family has dinner early so we're just about to sit down."

"Nice. How is Owen? Did he get you something perfect?"

Gabby rubbed her chest, over her heart. "He got me a few things, actually. But the best present has been spending it with his family. They're wonderful."

Min was silent for a second, and Gabby could hear

someone talking to her in the background. "Sorry about that. Wonderful, like *I want these people to be my in-laws* wonderful?"

Time to stop pretending, right? "Yes, actually. That would be the best present ever." And one she hoped wasn't too far in the future.

"If he breaks your heart, I break his face. Deal?"

Gabby shook her head. Maybe Min was connected. She was almost scarier than Wyatt. On a laugh, she replied, "Deal. I gotta go. Love you."

"Love you, too. See you soon. Tell dream-geek I said Merry Christmas."

"I will. Tell your family the same from me."

She stood in the hallway a moment, just listening to the chatter in the other room. It made her smile. Everyone was seated when she came back into the dining area. Owen stood when she walked in.

"I was just going to come get you."

She set her phone down, walked to her seat beside him. "Sorry. It was Min." She looked around the table. "She's my friend and my co-worker. She says Merry Christmas."

"Oh, you should have asked her to join us," Patty said.

Gabby laughed. "She has a gigantic family of her own. Her mother would never tolerate a missed Christmas."

Beth raised her wineglass. "Hear, hear. Sounds like a smart woman to me."

Owen laughed and sat down when Gabby did, smiling nervously at her. "Okay, Mom. Message received."

Patty said grace, which Gabby found heartwarming. While everyone had their heads bowed, she snuck a peek at each person and said a silent thank-you for the chance to be at this table with these people.

"Amen," everyone said together.

The food was passed and huge helpings were dished up. It smelled amazing, and Gabby figured the bounty rivaled whatever Min was eating. They chatted—or more accurately argued over which movie to watch after dinner. It still felt more like lunch to Gabby, even though it was the best Christmas supper she could remember having in far too long. She'd taken her last bite when Owen tapped his wineglass with his fork.

"Son, I think that means you're going to kiss your bride," Leo said. Everyone laughed and Owen's cheeks colored slightly. Gabby's stomach tumbled and her breath caught in her throat.

"Very funny, Dad. But I'd like to say something and in a weird way, it's sort of related to what you just said."

Now Gabby's breath evaporated completely. Her chest was a vacuum of space as Owen set his fork down and looked around the table at his family, his eyes settling on Gabby for just a second. He took a deep breath that she wished he'd share with her because she really couldn't catch her own. If her heart had tiptoes, it would be on them, pressed against her ribs, listening to hear the words she'd wanted Owen to say for so long.

"I have something to tell all of you," Owen said.

Everyone stopped eating, but it was Beth who spoke. "Is everything all right?"

Owen nodded. "Yes. Sort of."

His voice wavered and Gabby's brows scrunched together. *Sort of? What does that mean?*

Owen took a deep breath, let it out. "I've been lying to all of you and in doing so, I've made Gabby do the same. Which was not only cowardly and wrong, but unfair to her." Owen paused, looked at Gabby. "I owe it to you to be honest."

Oh God. He hadn't been lying to her, had he? About which part? Gabby's heart beat so loudly it was a wonder she could hear him. Would he tell her right this second, with an audience, that he loved her back? Butterflies grew giant wings in her stomach and flapped restlessly…happily. She gripped the edge of the tablecloth, squeezed the soft fabric between her thumb and finger.

Leo was easy to hear when he asked, "What are you talking about?"

Owen took another gulp of air. "Gabby and I are not and never were a couple. Everything you've seen between us has been…fake. A farce. I asked her to pretend to be my girlfriend because I'd lied about finding 'the one' and I didn't want to tell you guys."

Breath *whooshed* back into Gabby's lungs, almost choking her. *Everything you've seen between us has been fake. A farce.* Owen wasn't declaring his love. He was coming clean to his family to rid himself of guilt. For her. He thought this was what she wanted more than anything else. The truth. And he was being pretty damn clear about it. They weren't a couple. And never had been.

Owen cleared his throat. "We've never been in love. At least, not with each other." She could feel his eyes on her, but couldn't meet them. She couldn't look at any of them. He'd given her so much and was ripping it away from her. It felt like he was tearing her ribs out, one by one.

"I'm sorry. I'm sorry I lied and more, I'm sorry I asked Gabby, who really and truly is my best friend, to lie. She told me it would only lead to more lies and complications. And she was right. I thought it would be simple, but instead, it's just complicated everything. I'm hoping it hasn't lost me my best friend. Or the trust of my family."

Gabby's eyes darted upwards. Leo had his forearms crossed, resting on the table. Patty sat back, her arms also folded. Ophelia said nothing, but just stared in Owen's direction. Beth had tears trailing silently down her cheeks.

"Mom. I'm so sorry."

"Why? Why, Owen?"

He fidgeted beside Gabby. "No reason I give is good enough. It started because I was too chicken to tell you I hated all the noise and bluster of last year and the year before. I love all of you, love being with you. *This* has been the perfect Christmas, and I should have just told you how I felt, that crowds of people, especially people I don't know, stress me out. All I need to make the holidays is the people I care about. But in trying to get what I wanted, I hurt everyone I care for most."

He reached for Gabby's hand but she pulled away. She heard him whisper, "Gabs?"

"This is stupid, Owen," Ophelia said.

Gabby looked up. Her cheeks burned with embarrassment. With shame. She'd lied to all of these wonderful people. She'd done that, taken that leap, despite her own beliefs, because she loved the man next to her. And all it had yielded was half a dozen broken hearts.

"I'm sorry. Truly sorry," Gabby said, her voice rough, like sandpaper running over rocks. She'd let herself fall into a fairy tale and believe she'd come out victorious. Instead, she felt like the villain. The interloper.

"Why are you sorry?" Ophelia asked, looking genuinely surprised.

"Because it was wrong to lie just to avoid hurting some feelings and I should have stood stronger." She looked at Owen. It physically hurt to meet his eyes. "I should have told you no. All I want is for you to be happy, but I should have stayed true to myself. You have this beautiful family and they are a gift."

She looked around the table at all of them, pulling her

cloth napkin between her fingers. "You are a gift to each other. I know you're mad at Owen. You have every right to be. But I can tell you, with absolute certainty, that holding on to that anger and walking away carrying it in your heart could be the biggest mistake of your lives."

Gabby stood up, tossed the napkin on her plate. "Bigger than lying or playing pretend." She looked at Owen. "Bigger than pretending you don't love your best friend when he asks you to pretend that you do. Fight it out. Yell at each other. But don't for one minute leave here without realizing that I'd give anything," she said, pausing when her voice broke, "anything, to have what you all have. It started as a lie, but for me, every bit of it was real. More real than anything I've known in far too long. I'm sorry I lied, but I'm so grateful I got to be part of this Christmas. It was…everything."

There was nothing else she could say. She walked from the table, everyone breathing in stunned silence. She'd grabbed her phone and her purse by the time Owen rose from the table.

"Gabriella, wait. Hold on. Don't go like this."

She turned to face him, putting her hand up to stop him when he started to close the distance between them. "Don't. Please. I just need some time. I know you didn't want anything to change, O. But that's not life. Things change. I'm not saying we can't go back, that we can't be friends. I get that you weren't ready for the commitment of a ring, I really do. I can handle that. But it can't ever be the same." Because she couldn't look at him any longer, she looked around the table at each of them. Her gaze settled on Ophelia. "I'm sorry for my part in the deception. I hope you can all forgive me."

Without waiting to hear or see a response, she rushed out, biting back the tears until she crossed the hall and got to her own place. She struggled with the lock, then shoved the door open. When she slammed it shut, she realized she was shutting the door on everything she'd dreamed of having. Everything that, for just a tiny piece of time, she thought had been hers.

Falling back against the door, she sank down, pulling her knees up to her chest and letting the tears come. It was okay to mourn what was lost. It was the only way to heal.

Chapter Sixteen

Owen fought the urge to throw his plate across the room. What the hell had just happened? He'd started over, cleaned the goddamn slate, and everything he wanted had just walked out the door anyway. She *knew* about the ring. She *had* heard the conversation, which meant that Gabby lied to him. Though he had not one ounce of room to judge, the knowledge burned a hole in his gut. She'd lied to him and left without giving him a chance to say his piece. He was still standing, staring at the spot Gabby had just fled from, and realized his family was watching him. He turned, meeting the censure in their eyes head on.

He deserved it.

He thought it would be his mom or his dad that lit into him. He deserved that, too. He braced for it. But his dad hung his head, scooped up his last bite of turkey and potatoes and chewed silently. His mom picked up her wine and sipped. Patty followed suit. Dammit. He was such an idiot.

Ophelia was pulling her napkin from one hand to the other, the cloth slipping through her fingers. She tossed it on the table, picked up her wine, and downed the rest of the glass. Then she stood and walked to stand directly in front of him.

She poked him in the shoulder. "You are a goddamn idiot. Possibly the biggest idiot I've ever encountered. And trust me, I've known a few. We don't always see eye to eye and that's okay. Family has to love; they don't have to be the same. They have to accept differences and maybe put up with some quirks. But they don't goddamn lie and scheme like this. Who the hell are you? How could you do this? And more importantly, how could you do *that* to Gabby?" She pointed her finger toward the hallway. He started to speak, but she cut him off. "Whatever game you were playing, it might have been fake to you, but that girl loves you—and there is nothing fake about it. And on top of being a stupid lying ass to us, you were too blind to see it. You broke her trust and her heart for your own selfish gain because you weren't enough of a goddamn *man* to say 'hey Mom, I don't like so much noise at Christmas.'"

Owen's stomach dropped. His mother smacked her hand on the table. "Ophelia. Language."

Ophelia laughed angrily. "Right. By all means, let's be polite and sweet about this."

His dad stood. "You know, Owen, when you love people, all you want to do is be with them." His hands gripped the back of his chair and Owen felt a lump lodge in his throat. "I have a feeling you realize that more than you think. You just want to be around those people you love and if you have to make some adjustments, you don't mind. In fact, you're happy to do it." His eyes met Owen's and Owen felt like a child again, one who deserved his father's disappointment. "You might even spend your much needed vacation time traveling by train to visit your son in his fancy-ass apartment, simply because that's what makes the people you love happy. You know that, I think, because you'd do that for Gabby. A woman you've known for two years. A woman I think you're just realizing you love. But you've known us your whole life. How could you not think we'd do the same for you? Adjust to accommodate whatever it was that was holding you back?"

"I don't know." Owen's voice was gravelly. It hurt his throat to speak. "I'm sorry, Dad. I'm truly sorry. The only thing I wanted was a quiet Christmas and instead of asking for that, asking for exactly what I got, I lied to get it. I can't change that, but I can tell you I won't ever break your trust again."

His dad nodded, but said nothing else.

"And what about Gabby?" his mom said, not looking at him.

Jesus. Gabby. He couldn't live with what he'd done, what he'd missed, what had been staring him in the face this whole time. He'd been worried about telling her he wanted more, that he didn't want to go back to just being friends, completely oblivious to her feelings. Sure, he knew she was into him now, but she *loved* him. He hadn't wanted to say the words, not in front of people, because he hadn't wanted to scare her off. He thought his parents would leave, they'd ease over the threshold of friends to lovers, and then he'd tell her loved her.

He was supposed to *know* her. She was his person. He was hers. And he'd let her down so badly, he wondered if there was any way to salvage what they had. What he'd slammed a rock through and shattered. He took a step toward the door, fear crawling into his chest and sending a shiver down his spine.

"Leave her be, Owen," Patty said. Owen looked at her.

"Excuse me?"

She lifted her wineglass as if punctuating her words. "That girl gave you everything, asking nothing in return. Until two minutes ago. She asked you to give her time and it is, swear to God, the absolute least thing you can do. If you love her, give her that."

His shoulders sagged. He'd wanted to give her everything. But not this. He didn't want to give her time to realize he didn't deserve her. That he was an oblivious screw-up who couldn't see what was right in front of his goddamn face. But Patty was right. His whole family was. He looked around at all of them.

"I'm sorry. I'm sorry I wrecked Christmas."

His mother stood then and Owen didn't think there was any piece of his heart left to crack. But the sadness in her eyes proved him wrong. She walked to him, putting an arm around his waist and Ophelia's. "Christmas isn't over. At least we got our meal and presents out of the way. Let's clean up, we'll play cards. Maybe watch a movie. It's not over yet. Let's salvage what we can."

Owen shuffled his feet alongside his mom and prayed, with everything in him, that what she said could ring true for him and Gabby as well. It just couldn't be over.

Chapter Seventeen

Gabby had done three things when she'd finished sobbing on the floor: changed into pajamas—Christmas ones. Grabbed an actual bucket—well, large bowl—of snacks. And turned on the television to an all-Christmas-all-day channel. And then she did her best not to move. Because moving hurt. Thinking hurt. At the moment, even with Buddy the Elf on screen, even breathing hurt. She'd been so stupid and she hated that almost more than everything else. She knew the realities of life—how harsh and cold they could be. So why had she let herself think she'd get the guy in the end?

A knock on the door brought her out of her hazy cloud of pity. She glanced toward the sound but was reluctant to move. Another knock. She couldn't see Owen, yet. It had only been a few hours. Okay. Eight. But she couldn't see him. Pushing her fleece blanket off her lap, she set her chip bag on the coffee table and padded to the door. If it was him, she wouldn't open.

It wasn't. She saw Brady through the peek hole. "Open up, Gabs. I come bearing gifts."

She opened the door, knowing he wouldn't care about her

puffy eyes or pajamas. She tried to smile. "Merry Christmas."

He tilted his head and gave her a sweet half-smile that brought the lump back to her throat. Stupid Owen. Brady knew, which meant that one more person in her very small circle knew what an asshat idiot she was.

"You okay?"

She shrugged. "What's in the bag?" She pointed to the festive holiday bag he was holding.

He grinned. "Let me in. You show me mine, I'll show you yours."

Though it felt rough, like she was recovering from a bad chest cold, she laughed and moved out of the way, shutting the door behind him. They walked to the living room and she turned the volume down on the TV. Since Owen had her tree, she'd left a few gifts just wrapped on a side table. She grabbed Brady's and sat on one end of the couch. He sat on the other, looking at her expectantly.

"What did Owen say?" she asked.

Brady set the bag on the coffee table and Gabby tried to pretend she wasn't curious. "He didn't say anything. What the hell is going on? All he did was text me a dozen times begging me to check on you and said he'd explain later."

Tears stung. She practically tossed the gift at Brady and grabbed the one he'd brought for her. "Nothing is going on. I misread a situation because I'm stupid. I got what I deserved."

She'd started to tug at the tissue paper sticking out the top, but Brady shifted closer and gave her a side-hug.

"What's that mean? You're about the furthest thing from stupid I can imagine. And as to what you deserve, the list is endless."

She smiled, some of the sadness vacating her heart with his compliment. "Thank you. That's nice of you to say."

He squeezed her hand and then released it. "Not just saying it, Gabs. You're incredibly talented, funny, smart, and gorgeous. I don't know what's going on and I'm worried because I love you both. But I can tell you this, Owen could look the world over and never find a woman as great as you. So again, as to what you deserve? It's a hell of a lot."

A few tears slipped past and she wiped them away with her finger tips. "Thank you," she whispered. He had no reason to say it and even if it was hard for her to believe, *he* believed it. Which mattered.

"Open your gift. You'll feel better. I promise." He grinned like a little kid.

Gabby took out the tissue paper and found a carton of her favorite ice cream. She pulled it out, laughing. "This is perfect."

"There's more," he said, gesturing to the bag.

She dug in and found a coupon book that gave her twelve "one free ice-cream cone" tickets. For the first time since the day began, the pressure in Gabby's chest loosened and she laughed for real.

"Thank you. Absolutely perfect," she said again. "Let me put this in the freezer and then you can open yours." She brought a soda for him and settled back in her spot.

He tore open the wrapping and held up the dark blue T-shirt. He read the front and chuckled, his eyes smiling. "This is awesome. You have it made?"

She nodded. "Kind of. I drew your car and did the lettering then took it to a T-shirt design place." Brady loved his car and she'd written the caption MECHANICS KNOW HOW TO MAKE YOUR ENGINE PURR in block letters under it.

He leaned over and kissed her cheek. "I seriously love it. Thank you." He put it on the back of the couch and opened his soda, and grabbed her bag of chips. He leaned back, grabbing a handful of chips and shoving them in his mouth.

"I have some good news," he said when he finished chewing.

"Oh yeah?"

"Our screw-up building manager is history."

Gabby sat forward. "What? He was here yesterday."

"Yeah, but his apartment is cleared out. Something has gone down. I'm not entirely sure what, but it was enough to get him to leave. It's pretty obvious he was behind the thefts. Maybe all the cop presence spooked him. I got in touch with the building owner's daughter. Apparently she's in charge of daddy dearest's property, but she's overseas. Left her a few messages and she finally got back to me this morning."

Gabby's mind was buzzing. Apparently the world could continue to function even after Owen broke her heart. "It's good she got back to you."

He wiped his hands on his jeans and put the bag back on the table. "Yeah. She said she'd been in touch with one of the tenants and the police and assured me that Jake would no longer be an issue. Offered me a pretty sweet cut on my rent if I'd take over until she could get here."

"Wow. That's crazy. Obviously, you'll do it, but what about your shop?"

He shrugged. "I got guys working for me. I'll call a meeting and tell the tenants what's up. I am curious which of them she'd been in touch with, though."

"Yeah," Gabby said, her mind cataloging the options. It could have been any of them. "At least he's gone. You're way less creepy than him."

Brady picked a piece of chip off his shirt and tossed it at Gabby. "Really nice."

"Did you have a good Christmas?" she asked, covering a yawn.

"Good enough. Went to one of my mechanic's. His wife put on an awesome spread. I need to get going. I've got a side job I have to do tomorrow. Will you be all right?"

She nodded. What choice did she have?

She walked him to the door and sighed, leaning into him, when he pressed a kiss to her forehead. "You're both my friends, Gabs. I just want you to be happy. Don't give up on happy, yet, okay?"

She stepped back and nodded. Brady's lips tilted into a frown and then he added, "Or Owen."

Though her heart pinched painfully, she just nodded again. When he left, she straightened up and crawled into bed, all too aware of how big it felt with no one beside her.

Chapter Eighteen

Owen figured he'd felt more nervousness in the past couple weeks than he had in his lifetime. His family had left on the twenty-sixth—three days ago. His mother hadn't wanted to go without saying goodbye to Gabriella. He'd convinced her that he needed time to work on getting Gabby back, for good, and couldn't start until his family left. He also promised that whether he fixed things or not, he'd come home to visit for his birthday in January. He just hoped like hell he'd be visiting with Gabby.

Owen hadn't been able to sleep since Christmas night. He'd spent a lot of time thinking about his relationship with his best friend. He couldn't pinpoint the exact moment he knew he was full-on-head-over-heels-never-get-over-it-in-love with her because maybe a little part of him always had been. What he knew now was that if he couldn't get her back, if he couldn't fix what was broken between them, his life would never be the same. He'd given her a few days and he'd spent that time putting his home back in order and thinking about how to prove to Gabby they were more than friends. He didn't just want to date Gabby or sleep with her or make her laugh every day. He wanted to be her forever because regardless of what happened, she was his.

Brady had been over the day before to grab Gabby's canvas and paints. Owen had chickened out a dozen times already this morning, but he couldn't go any longer without seeing her.

He knocked on her door. It felt foreign to do so. There was no answer. He knocked again, more urgently. Where would she go? She didn't have to work today. Min's? He could call, but if he was wrong, Min would know something was up. For a tiny little woman, she could incite fear with just a look, and Owen knew he'd more than earned her wrath.

"Son of a—." He plunked his head against the door. He texted Brady: *Do you know where Gabby is?*

Leaning against the wall, he waited, growing more irritated by the second. He shouldn't have waited. He should have come over yesterday or the day before. He shouldn't have screwed things up in the first place.

Brady texted back: *Lose your girl again?*

Owen growled and pushed off the wall, pacing the hallway. *Don't be an ass. Do you know or not?*

Brady was swift. *Too soon? Sorry man, I don't.*

Owen's hand clenched on the phone. His stomach was a ball of knots tangled too tight. He needed to find her. He knew her. Where would she go? An idea popped into his head and because it felt right, because he needed to be right, he went with it. Hurrying back into his apartment, he grabbed his keys and a jacket. He'd find her—and he'd do it on the first try.

If he drove all over town looking, she'd never know. She'd only know that he found her. But for him, it was like a test, and if he failed, he'd question whether he deserved her; whether he knew her inside and out. Like she knew him.

The Museum of Fine Arts was an overwhelming structure. He didn't like being inside it—too much space, whereas Gabby felt the opposite. She liked the wide wings and open rooms. She preferred Degas and Monet, though she said their styles were different. For her birthday last May, he'd brought her here and sat beside her, absorbing the art with her. She said it was the best gift because the things she cared for most surrounded her. Art and him. How had he not known? His mind was a live wire, trying to think if she'd given signals of her feelings. But it was hard to catalog moments when they spent so many of them together.

Paying the full price to get in, even though there were only forty minutes until closing, Owen headed toward the stairs. One shot. He wouldn't stop if she wasn't there, but he'd know, in his heart, that he hadn't known her the way he wanted to, known her well enough to find her when she needed him. Even if, at the moment, she probably thought she didn't.

His footsteps were loud on the shining floor. There were more people than he expected. Reaching the second floor, he slowed his steps in an effort to catch his breath, to compose himself. On the wall beside Gabby's favorite room was a placard with a quote from Leonardo Da Vinci that read: *Don't choose the one who is beautiful to the world, choose the one who makes your world beautiful.* His heart was in his throat as he rounded the corner.

Owen's knees buckled, but he caught himself. Sitting in the middle of the room, she was a tiny figure, surrounded by greatness. To him, she was the most precious thing, the most beautiful, in the entire place. Other people milled about, but Owen only saw Gabby

Her slender shoulders were hunched as she stared at the wall. Gabby always told him she loved being the only one who knew where her pieces started. They began with one little mark and ended up filling the page. By the time people saw them, there was no end and no beginning; just her creation. And where she had started was her little secret. He wondered if she was trying to figure out that very secret in the works she studied, or if she was seeing anything at all.

He didn't know exactly when she'd become his whole world. All that mattered now was letting her know.

His feet were silent as he moved toward her. She didn't even startle when he sat on the bench. They said nothing at first, and he just listened to the sound of her breathing. It soothed him, the way he thought looking at the paintings might soothe her.

A quiet announcement said the museum would be closing soon. He did nothing to rush Gabby.

She didn't look at him when she spoke. "Every time I look at a painting I've seen a hundred times before, I notice something new," she said. He'd even missed her voice.

Owen stared at the Degas on the wall. He remembered thinking they were a lot smaller than he'd expected when she first brought him. He wasn't sure he could notice even a tenth of the things she did. Blue, gray, and black paint. Little bits of movement. Signature in the right corner. A woman's body in motion. But he knew she saw more. Gabby always saw more—not just what was on the surface, but everything underneath. Owen took her hand and realized, he might not have that ability with art, but he did with Gabriella.

Before he could tell her that, she spoke. "The thing that makes art so powerful isn't the technique or who the artist is. The power comes from the perception of the person looking at it. To me, this could be the most breathtaking image I've ever seen. It could make me feel alive and inspired and for you, it might just be a dancer."

He didn't know what to say. She turned toward him and because he couldn't *not* touch her, he reached for her other hand as well, grateful she didn't pull away.

Gabby kept her eyes lowered, staring at their entwined hands. "I could tell you everything about that picture. I could describe the history, tell you about the artist, tell you who inspired him and how he created it. But I could never make you love it the way I do. I can't make you see what I see."

He tightened his fingers and pulled her closer, his throat thick. Using one hand, he nudged her chin so she looked up. "I see. I promise you, I see." And once he cleared everything up, he'd never again let her feel invisible.

Tears surfaced and he wondered if he was too late. She sniffled. "What do you see, Owen?"

While he tried to gather his thoughts, she started to pull her hands away, but he held tight. "I see a woman who has come to mean more to me than I ever thought possible. A woman who makes me laugh, who makes me happy. I see someone so beautiful, inside and out, that it literally takes my breath away." He gestured to the painting. "When I'm with you, I feel like you do when you're looking at your favorite artists. And I also see I've been an idiot."

She gave a watery laugh and he was grateful that, despite the shine in her eyes, she wasn't crying. "I can agree there."

He stared at her. He needed a minute to do just that. She looked down at the floor and Owen felt her retreat. He'd wanted to do this right by telling her how he felt while showing her at the same time. Preferably at his place. But things didn't always go as planned and he wasn't walking away without telling her how he felt. He wasn't walking away, period. She stood and, before he could stop her, went to one of the paintings. Owen followed, not caring that more people had entered the room. He needed her to look at him.

"Gabby?" His voice was rough. He curled his fingers into his palms so he didn't reach for her. Again.

She glanced over her shoulder at him, just quick enough he caught the tears. If she'd kicked him in the stomach, it wouldn't have hurt any less than seeing her pain. "I thought it'd be okay. You know? Seeing you. And I think it will, eventually, but I just need a bit more time. I don't want to give up on our friendship. I can't do this right now, though." She kept her voice low, but every word felt shouted.

He shook his head. No. No more time. He'd wasted enough and he didn't want more. He stepped forward but stopped before they were touching. "No." His voice seemed to vibrate in the room. Some guy in a suit glared at him, but Owen ignored him. It was just him and Gabby.

Gabby turned to face him, her eyes flickering with anger. "Excuse me?"

"I'm going to do everything I can to convince you that we don't need more time. I don't want to go another minute without you. I need you and I want you, forever. And I want it to start right now. I love you, Gabriella." *Jesus, that feels good to say.* He felt almost boneless with the weight of that off his chest.

Her breath caught in what looked like a silent sob, and she pressed one hand to her chest. "Oh, I know you love me, Owen. I'm the best friend a guy could have, right?" Her laugh was jaded and didn't suit her. Didn't suit his Gabby. He felt the stares of a few patrons and his stomach rumbled with nerves. Unable to care any longer, he said what he needed to say.

"You *are* the best friend I could ever have," he said. She winced and he stepped closer. She pressed herself against the wall. A security guard cleared his throat.

"Can't be so close to the paintings, ma'am. Everything all right?" The guy stayed across the room but he was watching Owen. He took Gabby's arm and pulled her away from the wall and the painting. Sweat dampened the back of his neck. "We're fine, thanks." Another glance around the room proved that the guard wasn't the only curious observer. Several people had turned toward where he and Gabby stood and Owen's stomach felt like he'd eaten ten pounds of cotton candy. *It doesn't matter. Gabby matters. That's all.* Blocking everyone else out, swallowing down his nerves, he fastened his gaze back on Gabby.

"That's not what I meant. I meant I *love*-love you. Not just friend-love you. I'm in love with you. So in love with you that I don't know how I ever thought I wasn't. I want to be with you in every way. Yes, you're my friend—my best friend—but I want you to be so much more than that. I want to be the man who makes you laugh and wipes away your tears. I want to be your biggest champion and supporter. I want you to be mine. I want to make you sandwiches at midnight and order pizza when you forget to eat. I want to wake up beside you every single day. I want to go to sleep beside you every night. I want to make love to you and I want to cross every line and boundary left because I can't stand the thought of anything being between us."

Tears poured down her cheeks and he moved in, cupped her face in his hands, relieved that she didn't push him away. Owen was vaguely aware of strangers looking at them, but all he could really focus on was even though her hands stayed by her sides, she didn't retreat. "I love you, Gabby. Like I didn't know it was possible to love. I said I see you, but I didn't see everything before. I've been an idiot and it'll break something inside me if it's too late to fix it. To get you back. Not just as my friend, as my everything. Because that's what you are." He rested his forehead against hers, feeling his own throat thicken with emotion. "I see you, Gabby. You're everything to me."

Her silent tears made the moment longer and Owen felt like there was no oxygen in the room. His heart was pounding, his body was rigid. He didn't even try to breathe. Without Gabby, there was no point.

Then, as if he was dreaming, he felt her hands come to his waist, slide up his sides and down his arms until she was gripping his wrists. "I love you. I love you so much it hurts."

He wiped at her tears. "I don't want it to hurt. I'm so sorry I hurt you."

"You didn't mean to," she whispered.

"It doesn't matter if I meant to. I was careless with your feelings. And oblivious to my own. But I won't be anymore. I promise you. I promise you I can be the man you want."

She laughed and shook her head. "You already are."

He bent to kiss her, but stopped. "About the ring?"

Gabby's cheeks went a pretty shade of pink and she ducked her head.

He tipped it up with his index finger under her chin. "Gabs, that thing is all kinds of ugly and has really bad karma."

Her brows scrunched together like she might not believe him. She sniffed, then giggled. "I don't need a ring. I just need you."

"I just don't want you to think I'm not ready for commitment. I'm ready for everything. With you."

More tears filled her eyes and she nodded. Owen's hands were wet with her tears as he pulled her body up against his and kissed her, not for pretend, not for show, but because she was the most important, most genuine person he'd ever known in his life. And she was his.

Slow clapping started, breaking the moment as the sound and speed increased. When he pulled back, still holding her tight, he saw the small crowd had both watched and listened. Apparently, he'd put on a show after all. Gabby looked around and laughed, sniffling loudly.

Owen sighed and hugged her tight, burying his face in her hair. He whispered into her ear, "Can we finish this at home?"

She put her head back and laughed, then cupped his face in her hands like he'd done. His body ached with the need to be with her completely. She gave him a noisy, playful kiss. "Yes. Let's go home." The onlookers continued to clap as they left the room hand in hand.

As they descended the stairs, Gabby leaned her head on his arm. "I'm sorry I walked out and didn't say goodbye to your family properly. Brady said they left?"

He nodded, releasing her hand to wrap his arm around her shoulder. He couldn't get close enough. "They did, but they understood, and I assured my mom we'd visit next month."

Gabby arched one eyebrow. "Is that so? How'd you know I'd come around, that we'd be okay?"

He pushed open the door that led to the parking lot. "Because I wasn't going to give up until we were. It's the only thing that matters. Are we? Okay, I mean?"

He felt her shiver against his side. "We will be, I think. We probably have some things to work out, though," she said. When they reached his truck, he unlocked it, opening the door for her. Gabby looked up at him, her grin playful. "Like how soon you can get your stuff out of my new apartment."

Owen froze and not because of the night air. Putting his hands to her hips, he waited. Was she serious? He ran one hand through his hair. "I, uh…yeah. A deal is a deal. You still want to trade, huh?" It's not like he had any right to rush her.

She smiled coyly, tipping her head to one side. "Well, yeah. I earned it fair and square. Why? You don't want to trade anymore?"

Pursing his lips, Owen stared at her, trying to figure out if she was messing with him. "I won't renege if that's what you're asking. I was sort of hoping that we'd…that, uh…we'd—"

Thankfully Gabby cut him off, wrapping her arms around his neck and going up on tiptoe so their lips were almost touching. "Live together?"

He sighed deeply and rested both hands on her waist. "Yeah, actually. I was really hoping that."

"You can handle my messy?" she asked.

"I can handle anything, as long as I have you."

With a dreamy sigh that had her breath fanning his lips, she kissed him. When she pulled back, she whispered, "Then I guess we're okay. Because you have me. For good."

Epilogue

Owen was a vault. She'd wanted to surprise him for his birthday, but he insisted he had a plan. After ringing in the New Year together, quietly, with the glow of the firelight casting shadows over them, they'd settled into a routine. It was much like the one they'd had before becoming a couple, only now they spent every night together and Gabby was so happy she felt she might burst.

They'd spent the previous weekend at Owen's family's house. They'd been thrilled that he and Gabby were finally together for real and had been every bit as open and welcoming as they'd been through the holidays. Gabby could tell how pleased they were that Owen had come home to have a pre birthday celebration with them. But tonight, his actual birthday, was just for Gabby and Owen.

Gabby couldn't even get the tiniest hint from him about their plans, though, and it was driving her crazy. She should be the one doing something special for him. She'd stayed in her old apartment for the day to work and give Owen the space he cryptically said he needed. She'd paid the rent until the end of January so she figured it didn't hurt to move her stuff into *their* apartment at her own pace. When her alarm sounded, pulling her out of her latest piece, she decided she'd done enough for the day and went to get ready for her date. With the man she loved. The one who loved her back in exactly the same way.

Showered and ready to go by seven as the birthday boy had asked, she tamped down on the urge to go across the hall and ask if he was ready. Owen had insisted he'd come for her and not to sneak over. He knew her too well. When he knocked, a silly grin spread across her face. She walked to the door.

"Who is it?" she asked teasingly.

"The man of your dreams," he answered.

She pulled the door open, her breath catching when she saw him dressed in dark suit pants and a crisp white, button-up shirt. His three-quarter length gray wool coat hung open. His hair had a touch of product in it so it wasn't sweeping his forehead. He looked perfect. "You are, you know," she said, slipping her fingers into his waistband and yanking him close. "The man of my dreams."

Before he could reply, she kissed him. In her heels, their bodies and mouths lined up better, but she still had to reach for him. She kissed him as his hands came to her hair, his fingers tangling in the back of it as he pressed them closer, and he took over the kiss entirely. By the time he pulled back, Gabby had lost her breath. She looked at him feeling dazed and tingly from her head to her toes.

"You look stunning," he whispered against her mouth, nipping at her bottom lip and sending a shiver all the way through her body.

"So do you. Where are you taking me?"

"You'll see." He grabbed her coat, helped her into it, his fingers tickling the nape of her neck when he helped pull her hair out from the collar. He pressed a sweet kiss to her neck.

"I love you," he whispered.

She'd never get tired of hearing it or the feeling of believing it. She glanced up over her shoulder, meeting his gaze. "I love you."

They stepped onto the elevator and Gabby stared at him, unsure why he pressed the button for the roof. Gabby spent time up there in the summer. A few of the neighbors had put together a community garden that grew flowers, carrots, and some lettuce during the season. She'd painted up there a couple times. There was a small solarium in one corner that went mostly unused, a few benches, and a couple of wrought-iron bistro sets. It got far less traffic than it deserved in the summer and none in the winter.

Owen linked their fingers, smiling at her like he could see the wheels of wonder turning in her head. The elevator stopped and the doors slid open. Owen's hand reached the small of her back, nudging her forward. Snow covered the garden boxes and the cement except for a path that had obviously been cleared. Gabby shivered, looking around. The sky was lit by thousands of stars glittering above them.

More light came from the solarium as Owen led her in that direction. When he pulled open the door, she gave a small gasp of surprise. And pleasure. A small table was set for two. The glow of candlelight surrounded the space, using the thin, plank shelving that was meant for herb boxes. When the door shut behind them, the smell of rosemary and something decadent enveloped Gabby. Whatever they were eating was covered with silver tops, like they'd ordered room service at a fancy hotel. A couple of small, portable heaters glowed red, warming the space, making it intimate and cozy. She pressed her hand to her chest, felt her heart beat strong and steady. She turned and saw Owen was watching her.

"When did you do all this? How?"

He stepped closer, pulled her into his arms. "Did you really think I was working all day? Thankfully you were too caught up in your art to realize I was in and out of the apartment constantly. Not sure how I'll plan surprises once Brady rents your place out," he said.

Gabby laughed, delight filling her chest, her heart. "Maybe we should hang on to it. Just for moments like this."

A frown tugged at Owen's lips and his brows moved together. "That's not really financially responsible. There are—"

She rose up and pressed a noisy kiss to his lips, then held his face in her hands. "I was joking. This is wonderful."

He held her chair for her, waited for her to sit before he sat across from her. "I wanted tonight to be special. I know you were hoping to plan something for my birthday, but all I wanted was a date with the woman I love."

She smiled at him. "Well, you're getting that for sure. Your present is downstairs. Did you guess what it is?" She'd gotten him tickets to a computer-geek convention that he'd mentioned wanting to attend.

"No, but I'm curious. I love you, Gabby. And I realized all I need for my birthday, or any day, to be special, is to spend it with you."

Happy butterflies danced in her stomach. "This is perfect. *You* are perfect."

Owen lifted the lids off their plates and chuckled. "Let's hope you still think so when I make you alphabetize your movie collection."

Gabby laughed. She'd have a lifetime of this feeling with him, she realized. Laughter, happiness. There'd be times when the opposite was true—she knew all too well that life could pin her down and steal her breath. But they'd have each other, and that made everything seem so much more…possible.

"This looks delicious," Gabby said, breathing in the herb-roasted chicken. Tiny fingerling potatoes and sautéed vegetables completed the meal.

"I ordered from Vinetti's," he said, his eyes glowing.

"Which means you ordered triple-layer chocolate cake for dessert?" It was both of their favorites.

He nodded. "It *is* my birthday. It's in the fridge. We'll head down after dinner."

She picked up her fork and knife while he poured them each a glass of wine. Before she cut into her chicken, she stopped, sighed, and set down the utensils.

"You okay?" He set the bottle of white down between them.

"I've imagined moments between us, just like this one, more times than I can count or want to tell you. But I don't know if I ever really believed it would happen. That we'd be here like this. It's more than I could have ever hoped for."

His eyes softened and he reached out for her hand. "Because I'm more obtuse than I realized, I *didn't* imagine moments like this between us."

She frowned, but he squeezed her hand and continued. "But now, from the moment we kissed in your apartment that first time, I haven't been able to stop thinking about all the moments, big and small, that we'll have. That we'll share. Now that it's happened, I can't imagine what my life would be like if we hadn't taken this turn."

Emotion swamped Gabby, making her throat tight. "Well, your apartment would be cleaner," she said, giving a watery laugh.

Owen chuckled, let go of her hand. "That is true. But I wouldn't trade this for anything. I'm sorry it took me so long to see it."

She took a bite of chicken; sighed in pleasure. "You've done an excellent job of making up for lost time, so I forgive you."

He laughed and dug into his own meal. In the light of the moon, with stars and flickering candlelight twirling around them, they chatted about nothing and everything and Gabby was filled with a sense of peace unlike anything she'd ever known.

She was still feeling like the heroine of her own romantic movie when they floated down the hallway, back to their apartment. Owen slid the key into the lock while Gabby swayed, tipsy from wine and intoxicated with love.

When he held the door for her, she was looking at him, but when she turned, her breath caught in her lungs. The room was lit by what seemed like hundreds of votive candles. The overhead lights had been dimmed, and the fire danced slowly in the hearth.

She moved farther into the room, like she was floating into a dream. Music swelled softly. A silver bucket sat near the couch, filled with ice and a bottle of what she figured was champagne. The door *clicked* behind her and she whirled, throwing herself against him.

"Owen, this is beautiful. It's elegance and romance without having to deal with the crowds or the crazy. Like we're in our own posh hotel."

He kissed the top of her head, squeezing her tight. "A little bit of both of us."

"It's perfect."

"It's just the beginning."

Owen led her to the couch, giving her a playful push so she sat down. When he kneeled in front of her, she inhaled sharply.

He smiled. "Not yet."

His eyes were heavy lidded as he watched his own hands

slide up one calf, over the fabric of her pants, then around to her upper thigh and before trailing back down. When he reached her foot, he slipped off her heel and placed it under the coffee table.

Gabby was mesmerized. Their silhouettes moved with the same slowness on the wall, dancing in the flickering light. "How did you do all of this? There's no way you left this burning for the entire time we were eating dinner."

Looking up from removing her other shoe, he smirked. "I had a little help."

Gabby arched her eyebrows. "Oh?"

Owen put his hands on the cushions, on either side of Gabby, leaning toward her, and whispered, "Brady loves to help."

Gabby glanced around, trying to image Brady lighting all these little candles. She gave Owen a loud playful kiss. "You must owe him big time."

"Yeah. You could say that," Owen agreed. He placed feather-light kisses on her jaw and Gabby arched her neck. When his lips touched her ear, he whispered, "But it was totally worth it."

Gabby's heart pounded heavily—almost bursting with need to be closer, to show him how much she loved him.

Her fingers moved to his buttons, quickly unfastening them. She pushed the shirt off his shoulders, taking a second to appreciate the hot, smooth feel of his skin.

"Slow down," he whispered.

Gabby pushed off the couch so they were both on their knees, their bodies pressed together. "No. I don't want to."

Owen chuckled until her lips pressed against his chest and she removed his shirt completely. She put her hands on his sides and pulled him closer, her nails pressing into his skin. "Jesus. Gabby, let me catch up or it'll be over before it starts."

Giddiness swamped her. They would never be over, and

the truth of that washed through her. Slowing her movements, she pushed him until he lay back and she was over him, her pants bunching up as her legs settled on either side of his hips. With exquisite patience, she trailed her lips from one side of his chest to the other, then up the column of his neck. "Is this slow enough for you?"

His hands gripped her thighs, one of them travelling up, over her back, to her shoulders, until he was pulling her down so he could kiss her. His lips were soft, but there was nothing gentle about the kiss. He shifted, rotated them so he was over her, looking down at her, like he could see everything. Like he wanted everything.

She arched up, using her hands to bring his face to hers so she could give him all she had. They'd been friends for so long that when she'd realized her feelings had shifted, she had to work hard to keep it hidden. And now there was nothing to hide. His fingers found the zipper on her dress pants and the sound of it, the feel of the back of his fingers grazing her tummy, made her shiver. She shifted, helping him remove his pants and boxers. They had all night, but she couldn't wait any longer.

Gabby won the argument as to whether they'd go fast or slow, but as she stretched out on the blanket in front of the fireplace, she figured the victory had been shared.

"I can't stop asking myself how the hell I missed the chemistry between us." Owen's breathing was still labored and his slick skin was hot against Gabby's. Her head was nestled in the crook of his arm and her fingers traced small circles on his chest.

"Sometimes you're not very observant."

Owen laughed, pressing a kiss to her forehead. "I had a carefully planned-out seduction, you know."

Gabby snorted, burying her face against his chest to hide her giggle. "Of course you did. I would expect no less."

With a mock frown, he told her, "I still plan to carry it out, you know. Though I might need some time to recover first."

Gabby's cheeks hurt from smiling so hard. "Sometimes the best things are the ones you don't plan on or for."

He tucked a tendril of hair behind her ear. "Turns out those are the scariest ones, too."

She nodded. "I guess so. For you. The only thing I was scared of was you not knowing or knowing and never feeling the same."

"But neither of those are true. I do know and I do feel the same. I can't imagine my life, my world, without you in it. I want everything with you. I want the everyday quiet moments and I want the busy, messy ones. I want a family. I want a future with you."

Gabby was so used to painting her feelings, her words got stuck. Owen didn't appear to notice. He stretched his arm over to his pants, rifled around in them until he pulled out a small square box.

"Owen." Her heart pounded as he sat up. "We're naked."

Owen laughed, moved her to a sitting position, and then yanked the throw blanket off the couch and wrapped it around her. He pulled the blanket they'd been cuddling on around him.

"There. Now we're…mostly covered. And besides, you're the one who just said the best things aren't always planned. I'd thought to seduce you after."

With a somewhat teary laugh, Gabby said, "You still can, but it's your birthday. I'm supposed to give you presents."

Owen paused and met her gaze steadily. "I know exactly what I want."

Gabby's hands shook as she pulled the blanket tighter, and Owen opened the lid of the box. An oval diamond shimmered in the candlelight. Gabby gasped, covering her mouth with a shaking hand. His hands looked completely steady. His eyes never wavered. "I love you, Gabriella. You are my best friend and the greatest joy in my life. You *are* my life. You're what makes it full and exciting and beautiful. Even if you are a bit messy," he said, his eyes suspiciously bright. She knew he teased her to offset his emotion.

Gabby laughed. "I'll work on it," she said quickly.

"Don't," he said. "There's nothing to work on. I want you exactly as you are. For the rest of my life. This is a ring that suits you. It's timeless and elegant, and when I saw it, I knew it was made for you. Marry me?"

Owen pulled the ring from the box. Gabby was all but vibrating as she held her hand out. The platinum band was thin, etched with a faint and intricate lace-like design, like it was woven with wire delicate enough to match her hands. It was simple. Elegant. Perfect.

Gabby nodded because once again words weren't enough. He slipped the ring on her third finger and pulled her close. And though emotions clogged her throat, she managed to whisper, "I love you."

"And knowing that, finally *seeing* it, is everything."

Acknowledgments

It's hard to adequately express how grateful I am to be publishing my first book through Entangled. Thank you to Stacy and Alexa for being wonderful editors and giving me this chance. A special thank you to Stacy for dozens of emails that make me smile. Thank you to Fran, my agent. Meeting you, knowing this was in the works, was one of my favorite moments. Thank you for believing in me and always telling me to believe in myself.

Thank you to everyone at Entangled for the opportunity to work with the Bliss line. To Lisa Felipe, thank you for not laughing too hard during our phone call and for your enthusiasm. Thank you to my family…always to my family. Their happiness is contagious and I feel so grateful for the support and love you give me every single day. To Matt, for feeding me like Owen feeds Gabby. I love you. To Kalie and Amy: you think it's the other way around, but you both inspire me every single day.

Thank you to everyone who has shared my news, liked my posts, connected with me, or read my books. It's plural now and at one time, I didn't believe I'd ever publish. Thank you for standing by me through an awesome journey that I truly hope is just beginning. To the very patient and special people that keep me going every single day when it comes to my writing: Bren, Tara, Christy, Kara….to the Romance Chicks. It's just beginning; for all of us.

About the Author

Jody Holford lives in British Columbia with her family. She's unintentionally funny and rarely on time for anything. She writes multiple genres but her favorite is romance.

www.jodyholford.weebly.com

Find your Bliss with these great releases...

WRONG BROTHER, RIGHT MATCH
an *Anyone But You* novel by Jennifer Shirk

When matchmaker Kennedy Pepperdine gets trapped in an elevator with a handsome stranger, she confesses to him that her current boyfriend might not be as perfectly matched to her as she thought. Imagine her surprise, then, when that same handsome stranger turns out to be her current boyfriend's older brother...and she's stuck with him for the next week, visiting her boyfriend's family for Christmas. The more time they spend together, the more they each start to wonder if Kennedy's supposed "right match" just might be the wrong brother.

CHRISTMAS WITH THE SHERIFF
a novel by Victoria James

After fleeing her beloved small town five years ago, Julia Bailey is back to spend Christmas with her family. Returning is hard, but keeping the devastating secret about her late husband is even harder. Her place isn't in Big Sky Country any longer...but the more time she spends with the irresistible Sheriff who saved her once before, and his adorable little daughter, the more Julia starts wishing she could let go of the past and start a new life.

SNOWBOUND WITH MR. WRONG
a novel by Barbara White Daille

Worst. Day. Ever. After Lyssa Barnett's sister tricks her into reprising her role at Snowflake Valley's annual children's party, she doesn't think anything can be worse than squeezing into her too-small elf costume. Then tall, dark, and way too handsome Nick Tavlock shows up to play Santa…and an unexpected storm leaves them snowbound in the isolated lodge. Now Lyssa is trapped with the man who drives her crazy in more than one way. She needs to stay strong--and far way from the mistletoe. Or maybe she just needs a little Christmas spirit…

HER ACCIDENTAL BOYFRIEND
a *Secret Wishes* novel by Robin Bielman

Shane Sullivan has no intention of settling down—in fact, his job depends on it, and nothing's more important than his work. Still, he can't help but agree to Kagan Owen's pretend boy-friend scheme, if only to find out more about the mysterious beauty. But when every touch from her sets his heart and body on fire, he realizes playing an accidental boyfriend may be more than he bargained for—and more than he can give.

Made in the USA
Charleston, SC
22 October 2016